ALIEN INVADERS

Meet the ALIEN INVADERS!
Five awesome aliens have been
unleashed from the darkest corner
of the galaxy – and they're out to
destroy the universe!

Only Cosmo, a young boy from planet
Earth, has the power to stop them. Recruited
by the elite defence organisation G-Watch to
defend the galaxy, Cosmo must prove himself
and commence battle against the
deadliest aliens in space . . .

Don't miss any of the titles in the
ALIEN INVADERS series:

ROCKHEAD: THE LIVING MOUNTAIN
INFERNOX: THE FIRESTARTER
ZILLAH: THE FANGED PREDATOR
HYDRONIX: DESTROYER OF THE DEEP
ATOMIC: THE RADIOACTIVE BOMB

And look out for the ALIEN INVADERS
from the WRECKING ZONE:

KRUSH: THE IRON GIANT
JUNKJET: THE FLYING MENACE
MINOX: THE PLANET DRILLER
ZIPZAP: THE DYNAMO RIDER
TANKA: THE SONIC BOOM

ALIEN INVADERS

ROCKHEAD & INFERNOX

MAX SILVER

RED FOX

ALIEN INVADERS: ROCKHEAD & INFERNOX
A RED FOX BOOK 978 1 849 41698 6

Collection first published in Great Britain by Red Fox,
an imprint of Random House Children's Books
A Random House Company

This edition published 2012

Collection copyright © David Sinden, Guy Macdonald
and Matthew Morgan, 2012
Cover illustrations, map and gaming cards by Dynamo Design
Interior illustrations by Siku
Designed by Nikalas Catlow

1 3 5 7 9 10 8 6 4 2
ROCKHEAD: THE LIVING MOUNTAIN
First published in Great Britain by Red Fox, 2011
Text and illustrations copyright © David Sinden, Guy Macdonald
and Matthew Morgan, 2011

INFERNOX: THE FIRESTARTER
First published in Great Britain by Red Fox, 2011
Text and illustrations copyright © David Sinden, Guy Macdonald
and Matthew Morgan, 2011

The Random House Group Limited supports The Forest Stewardship
Council (FSC®), the leading international forest certification
organisation. Our books carrying the FSC label are printed on FSC®
certified paper. FSC is the only forest certification scheme endorsed by
the leading environmental organisations, including Greenpeace. Our
paper procurement policy can be found at
www.randomhouse.co.uk/environment

Set in Century Schoolbook

Red Fox Books are published by Random House Children's Books,
61–63 Uxbridge Road, London W5 5SA

www.kidsatrandomhouse.co.uk
www.randomhouse.co.uk

Addresses for companies within The Random House Group Limited
can be found at: www.randomhouse.co.uk/offices.htm

THE RANDOM HOUSE GROUP Limited Reg. No. 954009

A CIP catalogue record for this book is available from
the British Library.

Printed and bound by CPI Group (UK) Ltd, Croydon, CR0 4YY

CONTENTS

THE GALAXY

PLANET ZAMAN

TARN BELT

DELTA QUADRANT

GAMMA QUADRANT

PLANET ABU

PLANET OCEANIA

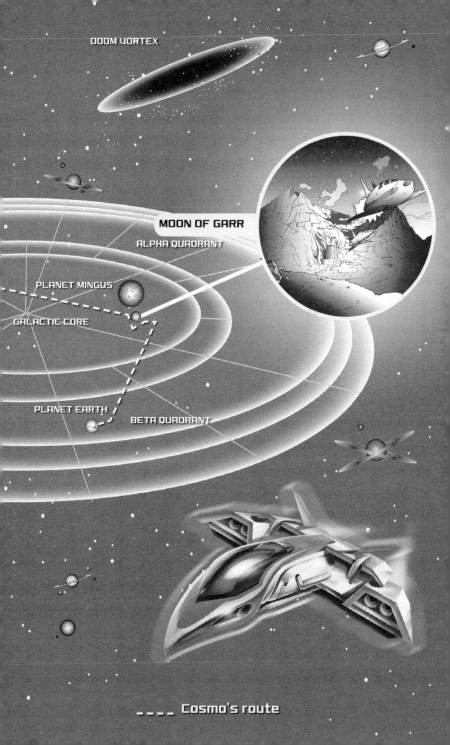

ATTENTION, ALL EARTHLINGS!

MY NAME IS G1 AND I AM CHIEF OF THE GALAXY'S SECURITY FORCE, G-WATCH. I BRING YOU GRAVE NEWS.

IT IS THE YEAR 2121, AND OUR PLANETS ARE UNDER ATTACK FROM THE OUTLAW KAOS. HE IS BEAMING FIVE ALIEN INVADERS INTO THE GALAXY, COMMANDING THEM TO DESTROY IT. IF THEY SUCCEED, THIS WILL BE THE END OF US ALL.

A HERO MUST BE FOUND TO SAVE US: ONE WHO WILL VENTURE THROUGH THE TREACHEROUS REGIONS OF SPACE; ONE WITH AN UNCOMMON COURAGE WITH WHICH TO FIGHT THESE INVADERS; ONE WHO POSSESSES THE POWER OF THE UNIVERSE! THAT HERO IS AN EARTHLING BOY. HE IS OUR ONLY HOPE.

ALIEN INVADERS

MAX SILVER

ROCKHEAD
THE LIVING MOUNTAIN

RED FOX

INVADER ALERT!

Deep in the galaxy, on a little-known
crimson moon, G1, the Chief of Galactic
Security, was working late. He wore
a golden spacesuit and stood before a
vast video wall inside G-Watch's secret
headquarters, checking the satellite
feeds. His silver eyes scanned the
incoming images: hovercars whizzing
through the Hwang metropolis, a space
station orbiting the planet Juno, a

convoy of freighters entering the Surian comet lanes. *No emergencies to attend to tonight*, he thought, relieved.

Suddenly the images flickered then froze as the satellite feeds jammed. G1's silver eyes widened with alarm as a new image of a hideous five-headed alien appeared on the video wall.

"Greetingsssss, G1," the alien hissed.

G1 folded his arms defiantly. "Kaos, you're spoiling my view."

The alien's five faces glowered at the Chief of Security. "This is your final chance, G1. Surrender the galaxy or I will unleash my forces."

The video image zoomed out, showing Kaos to be in the cargo hold of a large space battleship. Towering behind him were five monstrous aliens: one with a body of flames, another with fangs and spider-like legs, another with slimy writhing tentacles, one muscular and

glowing green, and one like a mountain of living rock.

G1 stared at the enormous aliens in shock.

Kaos's five faces grinned at him. "Meet Infernox, Zillah, Hydronix, Atomic and Rockhead. They're from the Doom Vortex, G1, and we've made a little deal together: I beam them into your lovely galaxy – and they destroy!"

"Kaos, I command you to stop!" G1 exclaimed.

But Kaos just laughed. "The galaxy will be mine, G1."

Rockhead, the enormous mountain-like alien, smashed his boulder-fists together. "*Destroy!*" he roared. Then the video wall flickered and the transmission ended.

The Chief of Security hurriedly unclipped a handheld communicator from his belt and spoke into it.

"G1 calling Agent Nuri."

A voice replied, "What is it, Chief?"

"The worst news imaginable," G1 said. "Kaos is sending in invaders from the Doom Vortex, commanding them to destroy our galaxy."

"From the Doom Vortex! But they'll be unstoppable, Chief!"

"We only have one hope. Fetch the Earthling at once."

"But Chief, he's still just a boy."

G1 looked up through a porthole into a starry sky. "We must hope he's ready. The future of the galaxy depends on him."

CHAPTER ONE

LEAVING PLANET EARTH

"The spaceship won't have left, will it, Mum?" Cosmo asked.

"We'd better hurry, Cosmo," his mum replied, rushing him in through the entrance of Heathrow Spaceport. They hurried across the concourse, pushing through crowds of people catching flights around the galaxy: families going on holiday to the paradise planet of Oceania, backpackers travelling to the

Wild Worlds, and businessmen attending conferences on Megatroplia. There were aliens coming in too, visiting Earth or catching connecting flights to other planets. Cosmo and his mum hurried past a family of long-nosed Lavadians carrying their luggage on their heads. Cosmo dashed through the legs of a Mollaxian as tall as the entrance hall, and squeezed between bulbous Gloopons eating burgers from the airport café.

He glanced at his reflection in the café's window and saw that his rucksack was half open, with a T-shirt hanging out – he'd packed in such a rush! He was wearing odd socks, one green and one red, and his wavy brown hair was unbrushed. *Oh, I wish I hadn't overslept*, he thought. He'd been so excited about the trip that he'd stayed up late asking Mum question after question about the galaxy.

It was the year 2121, and Cosmo Santos, an eleven-year-old Earthling, was off on his first trip to space. He'd won the lucky ticket in *Space Explorers,* an inter-planetary magazine. Thirty ticket-winners from different planets were off on a month-long tour of the galaxy!

Cosmo and his mum hurried into the departures lounge and checked the latest flight information on the electronic board:

LUNAR EXPRESS - PROCEED TO BLAST BAY 6
OCEANIC ORBITAL - DELAYED DUE TO SOLAR STORMS
MARS SHUTTLE - PROCEED TO BLAST BAY 18
GALAXY TOUR - BOARDING BLAST BAY 20

"Galaxy Tour – that's me, Mum!" Cosmo said excitedly.

They rushed through the crowd, heading for a long travelator marked BLAST BAYS 15–30.

"Excuse me . . . Sorry . . . Pardon me . . ." Cosmo and his mum hopped onto the travelator and it whisked them off like a conveyor belt, delivering them to BLAST BAY 20.

Cosmo saw a flight attendant at the bay's boarding gate. She had the cat-like eyes of an alien from Planet Kline.

"Ticket, please," she said.

Cosmo took a silver ticket from his jeans pocket and handed it to her. He waited excitedly as she ran her scanner finger over it.

"Welcome, Cosmo Santos, *Space Explorers'* winner from Earth," she said. "Looking forward to the tour, are you?"

"You bet!" Cosmo replied.

"Then let's get you on board."

As the attendant opened the boarding gate, Cosmo glanced out of the blast bay's window, spotting a silver spaceship on the launch pad outside. *A Type-3 Cruiser – brilliant!* He'd flown one before on a computer game that his dad had given him called *Flight Simulator Pro*. Type-3s were fast! They had twin thrusters and hyperdrive capability. In the cockpit he could see its android pilot checking the controls.

Mum smoothed Cosmo's hair. "Goodbye then. I'll see you in a month," she said.

Cosmo looked up at her. "I'll miss you, Mum."

She smiled. "I wish your father could see you now."

"Me too," Cosmo said, and he gave her a hug.

"Mr Santos, if you'd like to follow me, we'd better be on our way," the flight attendant called from halfway across the boarding bridge.

Cosmo hurried after her to the cruiser's door and it slid open. He took a last look back at his mum, who was waving from the boarding gate. He waved too, then followed the attendant aboard.

Inside the cruiser, the other competition winners were already seated in travel pods, each of them an alien from another planet. Cosmo followed the flight attendant past them down the aisle, recognizing some of their species from *Alien Encyclopaedia*, an old e-book of his dad's. He noticed a Baluvian man with webbed hands sipping a can of Raiderade, a six-armed Krucian woman reading six copies of *Space Explorers*, and a Mervish man wearing four pairs of sunglasses to shade his eight eyes.

I wonder if I look as weird to them as they do to me, Cosmo thought.

The flight attendant stopped at an empty pod halfway down the cruiser. "This one is yours, Mr Santos."

"Thank you," Cosmo said, and he flopped down into the large cup-like seat. It had an entertainment console and a viewing sphere to see out of the side of the ship.

"You'll find a wordsworm in the arm compartment of your seat," the attendant told him. "The rest of the tour group might be a little difficult to understand without it!"

Cosmo glanced around at all the passengers, hearing them speaking to one another in alien languages. As the flight attendant moved away, he flipped open the arm compartment and saw a small orange worm wriggling in a dish.

A girl in the pod opposite spoke to him. "*Ning den. Voola pip-pip*," she said. She wore a red spacesuit and had aqua-blue skin and pointy ears.

"Hang on a second – I can't understand you," Cosmo replied. He picked up the wordsworm and felt it wriggle in his fingers. Carefully he slid it into his ear and it burrowed down deep.

The girl spoke again and sounded completely different. "I said, 'It tickles at first but it's harmless,'" she repeated.

The wordsworm was translating her words as she spoke!

"We've got a pet one of these worms at school," Cosmo said. "And Mr Marshall, my Space Studies teacher, says it knows over twenty million galactic languages."

"You're native to Earth, I take it," the girl said.

"Yes," Cosmo replied. "This is my first trip to space. What planet are you from?"

"Etrusia in the Eagle Nebula. But I've been to many."

At that moment an announcement came over the passenger intercom. It was the android pilot speaking: "*Could all passengers please ensure that your luggage is stowed beneath your seats. We are preparing for blastoff.*"

Cosmo stuffed his rucksack into a

compartment at the base of his pod. "Here we go," he said to the Etrusian girl opposite.

"I hope you're ready for an adventure," she replied.

"You bet."

The girl smiled, then looked away through her viewing sphere.

Cosmo glanced out from his, and saw the boarding bridge disconnect; then, over the intercom, the android pilot commenced countdown: "*Ten . . . nine . . . eight . . . seven . . .*"

Cosmo felt the launch pad rising and tilting, moving the cruiser through ninety degrees pointing up to the sky. He was now lying on his back in his seat. The engines began rumbling, louder and louder.

"*Five . . . four . . . three . . .*"

Cosmo felt his seat trembling.

"*Two . . . one . . . blastoff!*"

Suddenly the twin thrusters ignited, and fire filled the viewing sphere. With an almighty roar the space cruiser powered upwards into the air. The force was immense, causing the whole ship to rumble and pushing Cosmo back in his seat as it shot through the clouds. Cosmo had never travelled so fast before; in moments the cruiser had reached the edge of Earth's atmosphere, its fins glowing red-hot from the speed. All at once his viewing sphere darkened, and Cosmo saw the dotted lights of stars. He glanced back and saw Earth getting smaller behind him. It felt awesome. He was in space! *See you soon, Mum*, he thought, and he smiled as he sped off into the galaxy.

While Cosmo was looking out of the viewing sphere, unbeknown to him the blue-skinned Etrusian girl in the pod opposite unclipped a handheld communicator from her belt. She pressed its transmitter and whispered into it.

"This is Agent Nuri. The Earthling boy is on his way."

"Time is pressing," a voice replied. "Begin the Crash Test."

"But, sir—"

"No 'buts', Agent Nuri. The boy will have the skills. The question is, will he use them – does he *really* possess the power?"

CHAPTER TWO

DANGER AT HYPERSPEED

As the cruiser flew through space, Cosmo felt himself floating off his seat in the zero gravity. He flicked a switch on his pod, activating its personal regravitator, and it pulled him back down. Drops of Raiderade from the Baluvian man's drink floated through the cabin, and he opened his mouth, catching one. It tasted like banana.

The cruiser passed the Moon; so close that Cosmo could make out the lights of lunar settlements. He saw other spaceships flying through the darkness: space freighters, Mars shuttles and delivery rockets. The cruiser's android pilot spoke over the intercom: *"Attention, all passengers. We are about to enter hyperdrive. Sit back and enjoy the flight."*

Through the viewing sphere, Cosmo saw that they were approaching the beacons of a space hyperway, one of the high-speed routes through the galaxy. The cruiser accelerated and the stars turned to long white streaks. They were travelling at hyperspeed, blasting across star systems faster than the speed of light.

Cosmo settled into his pod and checked out its entertainment console, flicking through the 4D movie channel and alien cartoons. He played two games of *Stargon Superhero* and tried the tasty in-flight snacks: meteorbites and burgerbombs, washing them down with Raiderade.

This is the way to travel, Cosmo thought happily, and he leant back, looking out at the streaking starlight.

Cosmo took a tattered photograph from his pocket. It was of his dad in the cockpit of a Dragster 5000 spaceship. Cosmo's dad had worked in space for the galactic security force G-Watch and Cosmo longed to be a G-Watch agent one day, just like him. *I miss you, Dad*, he thought. More than two years ago Cosmo's dad had died in a space-crash, and Cosmo still thought about him every single day.

Suddenly the cruiser shuddered, and Cosmo glanced up from the photograph. He saw the Etrusian girl in the pod opposite, her blue skin looking pale with fright. "What was that shudder?" she asked.

"We probably just changed hyperlane," Cosmo replied. "We're travelling at over eight hundred million miles per hour."

But then the cruiser shuddered again, dipping and swerving violently.

Cosmo heard the android pilot over the intercom: *"Could all passengers stay ininininin . . . Error . . ."*

The android pilot sounded strange . . .

"Errooor . . . terminaaaate . . . shutdoooooooooooooown."

Something's wrong! Cosmo thought.

The cruiser veered violently off the hyperway and came out of hyperspeed. He looked through the viewing sphere: they were heading straight for a huge planet made of shining liquid metal. Passengers started panicking, and an alien with stalked antenna eyes looked round from the pod in front, terrified.

The flight attendant's voice came over the intercom: *"Attention, all passengers. This is an emergency. Our android pilot has malfunctioned and we've lost control. Can anybody on board fly this spaceship?"*

Passengers screamed, fearing for their lives.

"*If anyone can save this ship, please step forward now.*"

Cosmo looked around. No one was stepping forward. All the passengers were gripping their pods, screaming at the tops of their voices. *Someone has to do something or the cruiser's going to crash*, he thought. He remained calm, strangely calm; inside him a feeling was growing – whether it was courage or foolishness he couldn't tell, but it was like a force, making him want to stand up and volunteer, even though he knew it would be crazy. *I've flown a Type-3 Cruiser on Flight Simulator Pro*, he thought. *It's not real flying, but it's better than nothing*.

He switched off his pod's personal regravitator and floated upwards, pulling himself along the cabin's ceiling towards the cockpit.

"*I'll* do it!" he called. All the passengers were staring at him.

"The Earthling's going to save us!" cried a Sterovian man.

Cosmo's heart was thumping. He dared not tell them the truth: that he'd never flown a *real* spaceship before.

He pushed open the cockpit door and saw the flight attendant examining the android pilot, the control panel on its back open. She turned as Cosmo floated in. "I can't get it working!" she said.

Up ahead, through the cockpit's space-screen, Cosmo saw the liquid metal planet getting larger by the second. He glanced at the cruiser's controls and recognized them from *Flight Simulator Pro*!

I can fly this ship, he realized. "Check on the passengers," Cosmo told the flight attendant. "I think I can save us!"

CHAPTER THREE

THE TEST

While the flight attendant stowed the
android pilot at the back of the cockpit
and went to check on the passengers,
Cosmo strapped himself in. *It's down
to me*, he thought as he took hold of the
steering column. He turned it hard to the
right, but felt the cruiser struggling to
realign. It was being drawn towards the
liquid metal planet.

"Planet Mingus is also known as the

ship-swallower," a little voice said. "It's magnetic."

Cosmo noticed a small bug-like robot staring up at him from the control desk.

It bleeped. "If we get any closer, it will suck us right in and we'll melt into it."

We need more thrust, Cosmo thought. He reached for the left thruster and fired it, swinging the cruiser free of Mingus's pull. "Er, thanks. Who are you?" he asked.

"I'm Brain-E, pilot's mate," the little robot replied.

"I'm Cosmo Santos."

"Well, Pilot Santos, I commend you on your bravery. Might I suggest you make an emergency landing on Garr? It's the moon that orbits Mingus."

Cosmo looked up through the space-screen and saw a tiny crimson moon above the metal planet. He aimed for it.

"As you enter Garr's atmosphere you'll need to be travelling at no more than four vectrons or we'll burn up," the robot said.

Cosmo glanced at the speedometer: *Eight vectrons!*

I need to slow us down – fast, he thought. He scanned the control desk looking for the switch that closed the fin vents.

The robot bleeped. "Where did you learn to fly?" it asked.

"Um . . . using a computer program my dad gave me. It has different spacecraft you can select." *Think, what closes the fin vents on a Type-3 cruiser? Ah, got it!* Cosmo flicked a switch on the side of the steering column and heard the hydraulic vents closing on the cruiser's fins. Garr was looming large in the spacescreen. *Seven vectrons . . .* The spaceship was slowing, but not enough. Cosmo felt the ship shudder violently as it met Garr's atmosphere. *Six vectrons . . .* He could barely keep hold of the steering column as

the cruiser shook and rattled under the
pressure of the rapid entry . . . *Five
vectrons . . . Still too fast,* Cosmo thought
desperately. *We're going to break up!*

The cruiser's nose-cone glowed red-hot from atmospheric friction. Sweat was pouring down Cosmo's face. He pulled back on the steering column, reducing the entry angle, doing whatever he could to slow the cruiser down . . . *Four and a half vectrons . . . four and a quarter* . . . His arms were shaking; the ship's spacescreen was now glowing with the heat . . . *Four vectrons!*

The cruiser roared into Garr's crimson sky. He'd made it through! Far below he saw an alien landscape of scarlet mountains. Garr looked bare and desolate. He saw peaks lit by the glare of Planet Mingus, and canyons deep in shadow.

"Turn fifteen degrees west for the landing site," the little robot said.

As the cruiser descended, Cosmo turned the steering column. He checked the ship's height on the altimeter: *3,000 metres . . . 2,600 metres . . .*

Cosmo tilted the cruiser, flying down among the mountains and banking between two peaks. Below, he saw a long straight canyon to land in that was free of boulders and rocks. He smiled. *This is way better than* Flight Simulator Pro*!* he thought.

Cosmo felt for a lever at the base of the control desk. "Lowering the landing gear now," he said to the little robot. He pulled the lever and heard a deep clanging sound.

"Perfect," the little robot said. "Bring us in nice and steady."

As the cruiser descended into the canyon, Cosmo pulled the steering column back slightly, raising the nose-cone. He braced himself for landing – *three . . . two . . . one . . .* The spaceship's back wheels touched down with a bump; then its front wheels bounced a little and skidded, throwing up plumes of amber dust. Cosmo

turned two red handles, and the air
brakes roared. The wheels screeched and
the cruiser slowed to a standstill at the
very end of the canyon. Cosmo breathed a
huge sigh of relief. He'd done it – he'd just
landed a Type-3 cruiser on an alien moon!
All the passengers were safe!

"Well done, Master Cosmo," the little robot said. "Nice flying!"

Cosmo smiled. *We've made it!* He leaned back in his seat and looked through a porthole: he noticed the exit ramp being lowered from the side of the cruiser. The flight attendant and passengers were leaving the ship.

Brain-E bleeped. "Why don't you join them, Master Cosmo? It's perfectly safe to go outside. On Garr, gravity is nine over zero, the temperature is warm and the oxygen is plentiful."

Cosmo left the cockpit and peered out from the top of the cruiser's exit ramp. He felt hot air on his face and saw the metal planet Mingus in the sky. Then, as he walked down the ramp, the other passengers started clapping.

"Well done! The Earthling's a hero!" they cheered, then crowded round, shaking him by the hand.

Cosmo spoke to the flight attendant. "So what are we going to do now?" he asked her.

She smiled, and the crowd parted. Cosmo saw the blue-skinned Etrusian girl who'd been in the pod opposite coming towards him.

"What happens next depends on you, Cosmo Santos," she said.

"On *me*?" Cosmo asked. "What do you mean? And how do you know my name?" He was sure he hadn't told her.

"Sorry, but not everything here is as it seems," the girl said. "The emergency landing – it was a set-up, a test."

Cosmo looked at her, confused.

She pointed up at the space cruiser. "Take a look up there," she said.

Cosmo saw the android pilot back in its seat, waving from the cockpit.

"The pilot didn't really malfunction. It was a test to see if you *really* had it in

37

you," she explained. "We wanted to know that you're ready. And you sure are!"

Cosmo stepped back, bewildered. "What's going on? Ready for what?" he asked.

The girl smiled again. "For G-Watch service," she told him. "The *Space Explorers* galaxy tour was a plan hatched by G-Watch to get you here in secret."

Cosmo looked around, seeing all the passengers smiling at him.

"My name is Agent Nuri," the girl said. "And everyone here works for G-Watch." She pointed across the canyon to the tallest of the mountains. "We've landed here on purpose. Over there is G-Watch's secret headquarters."

Cosmo squinted, seeing steps carved into the sheer rockface. Two enormous slabs of rock were sliding apart like doors. His mind was racing. "G-Watch? I'm really at G-Watch? This isn't a galaxy tour at all?"

"That's right," the Etrusian girl said.
"G-Watch needs you. Come inside and I'll
explain everything."

CHAPTER FOUR

G-WATCH NEEDS YOU

Cosmo followed Agent Nuri up the stone
steps to the entrance in the mountain.
He felt excited and puzzled all at once.
He'd thought he was coming on a galaxy
cruise, and now here he was, entering
G-Watch headquarters. *What could
G-Watch want with me?* he wondered.

At the top of the steps Nuri led Cosmo
inside. In a cavernous room, he saw
scientists working – testing vehicles

and gadgets. The room was full of space buggies, hyperspeed engines, satellites, tanks, interstellar probes and even a solar-powered rocketship.

"Wow!" Cosmo said, trying to take it all in. "This place is so cool!"

"G-Watch headquarters have been based on Garr for hundreds of years, Cosmo," Agent Nuri said. "Top-secret work goes on here. It's the perfect hideaway; no spaceships come because it's so close to Planet Mingus."

Cosmo saw the G-Watch agents from the space cruiser coming in too, some rushing to workstations and others disappearing through dark doorways.

"But why am *I* here?" he asked.

Nuri smiled. "All will become clear if you follow me."

She led the way through the room and Cosmo looked around in wonder. He watched a mechanic testing the hydraulics of a gleaming silver space plough. It was huge.

"That's the new X1 Indestructible," Nuri explained. "It can power directly through asteroid storms."

They passed a scientist at a computer station setting the time on his watch. Cosmo saw it flashing blue, then it glowed, and the scientist whizzed into the air and vanished.

"Where did he go?" Cosmo asked Nuri.

"He's testing a prototype navicom," she replied. "It's an experimental technology we're trying to develop for transporting agents in emergencies." She glanced at the scientist's computer screen. "Oops, I don't think it's working properly yet. It looks like he's beamed himself into an asteroid belt!"

She led Cosmo across a section of floor marked with a grid. As he followed her, he found himself trekking through

holographic landscapes: a steamy
rainforest, then a freezing snowdrift,
then a bone-dry desert. "What's this?"

"This is called the holodeck," Nuri
said. "It's the latest in virtual reality –
for training agents on how to survive in
hostile environments." She stepped to a
rack of hoverboards and took two down.
She hopped onto one and slid the other
over to Cosmo. "You do know how to
hoverboard, I presume."

"Of course," Cosmo replied. His dad had taught him and at school he was captain of the hoverball team – a sport played on hoverboards.

"Then follow me," she said. "It's the best way to get around."

Cosmo stepped onto his hoverboard and pressed his back foot down. The board began zooming upwards like he was surfing. He tilted left, veering round the solar rocket, then followed Nuri up past a

storm satellite and through an opening in the stone ceiling to a level above. It was full of G-Watch spaceships: starfighters, microjets and stealth drones. *Wow!* Cosmo thought. Some had their thrusters burning as G-Watch scientists and mechanics tested them.

"The G-Watch spacefleet is always ready," Nuri told him. "These fly out on rescue missions in the event of galactic emergencies."

Cosmo noticed a mechanic examining the engine of a white spaceship with laser cannons set into its nose. "Hey, is that a Dragster 5000?" he asked, surfing closer to take a look. "My dad flew one of these! He was a G-Watch agent. Did you know him, Nuri?"

"Not personally," Nuri replied. "But I have heard of him – James Santos, I believe."

"Yes, that's him."

"Well, this is a more recent model than he would have flown – the Dragster 7000. It's the most advanced G-Watch spacecraft to date."

Cosmo ran his hand along its gleaming hull. *This is my kind of spaceship*, he thought. *It's amazing!*

"Follow me," Nuri said briskly. "There's something that I need you to see a few levels up."

Cosmo followed her up through the levels of G-Watch headquarters, through a room containing a platoon of armed G-Watch battle-droids, then a surveillance room with a video wall and agents working at control desks.

Nuri stopped inside a white room with a tinted-glass cabinet and two large objects hidden under plastic sheets. "This is what I wanted to show you," she said. "It's top-secret."

Pulling off the first sheet, Nuri

revealed a deep-space reconnaissance probe squashed to a slab of metal. It had a clawed footprint as big as a man pressed into it. Then Nuri removed the second sheet, revealing half of a twisted G-Watch satellite. Buried in it was a razor-sharp fang as long as Cosmo's arm. Cosmo stared in shock.

"These were recovered from far beyond our galaxy, in the Doom Vortex, Cosmo. Both have been savagely attacked."

Yikes! Cosmo thought. "By what, Nuri?"

"By aliens of unimaginable evil."

Cosmo gulped, feeling shaken by what Nuri was saying.

"You won't have learned about these aliens in Space Studies at your school. These fearsome creatures have evolved in the most hostile outer regions of the universe. It's only in recent years that they've been discovered."

Cosmo stared at the clawed print and the fang, trying to imagine the fearsome aliens they'd come from. "But why are you showing these to me?" he asked, puzzled.

"Because five such creatures are coming to destroy our galaxy, Cosmo. They take orders from an outlaw called Kaos, and we need *you* to stop them."

CHAPTER FIVE

THE POWER

Cosmo stared in shock at the crushed
reconnaissance probe and the large fang
buried in the satellite. "You seriously
want *me* to fight enormous aliens? Are
you crazy?!" he asked Agent Nuri.

"Not crazy at all," she replied. "G1 will
explain."

The air shimmered and, as if by magic,
a man in a golden spacesuit appeared.
"Thank you, Agent Nuri," he said.

Cosmo blinked, startled. "Where did you come from?"

The man looked down at Cosmo with kind silver eyes. "Welcome, Cosmo. My name is G1, Chief of G-Watch, and I have much to tell you should you choose to accept your mission."

"But why me?" Cosmo asked.

"Because of who you are and what's inside you," G1 replied, eyeing Cosmo seriously. "Inside you, we believe there to be a unique power. What made you step up to save the space cruiser from crashing?"

Cosmo remembered the urge he felt before he volunteered to save the cruiser. "I only did what I thought was right," he replied.

"We believe you were drawing on something special inside of you, Cosmo – a power that's present in all life forms, but in you to an exceptional degree.

It can manifest itself as courage, honour, truth and even intense physical energy."

"I was just being me," Cosmo said, stunned. "I don't have any superpowers."

G1 smiled warmly. "Not a superpower like in stories, but a real power. It's the power of the universe, Cosmo."

Cosmo stepped back, stunned.

"Other people have noticed it too," G1 continued. "I knew your father, Cosmo. He was our greatest agent, and he alerted us to something special in you. We have been keeping watch over you from space for several years now, monitoring your progress with interest."

"Monitoring me? Why?"

"Should you one day choose to join us here. Your father has already trained you in rudimentary agent skills, Cosmo. Did you not realize?"

"Trained me?"

G1's silver eyes twinkled. 'You can fly any spaceship. *Flight Simulator Pro* is no computer game; it is a G-Watch training program. You can hoverboard, ski, scuba dive, and most of all you think like an agent, instinctively knowing the right thing to do."

Cosmo thought of his father, remembering all the brilliant things they'd done together. *So Dad was teaching me to be a G-Watch agent all along!* he thought, amazed. But he still felt apprehensive.

"Surely I can't fight these huge invaders," Cosmo said. "Can I?"

"You have the power, Cosmo," G1 said simply. "It is stronger in you than in any other. You are our only hope."

* * *

Meanwhile, deep in the Doom Vortex, battleship *Oblivion* was anchored behind a dead star. Kaos paced inside its cockpit, his five heads locked in debate.

"We must strike where it hurts," one head said to his others.

"We must destroy their fuel supplies and hijack their trade routes," another head added.

"We'll spread disease, fear and panic."

"The galaxy will beg for mercy!"

"G-Watch must suffer first. Without them to protect the galaxy, every star, planet and moon will be ours for the taking. Send in Rockhead, the living mountain!"

His five heads all cheered at once. "Send in Rockhead!"

A scrawny purple rat squeaked from the cockpit floor and Kaos's heads peered down at it. "Don't just stand there, Wugrat. Fetch the navicom."

The rat scurried to a metal shelf and took down a small crystal disk, holding it in its mouth. It scampered after Kaos down a long corridor.

The alien was chuckling to himself. "The secrets to the navicom transporter unit are ours," one head said.

"G-Watch is no match for us," another smirked.

Kaos opened the door to the cargo hold. Inside, five fearsome aliens were waiting.

"So, you wish to leave the Doom Vortex, eh?" Kaos said to them. "You know the deal. I beam you into the galaxy, and you fight for me."

"Yes, master!" the aliens roared.

"Rockhead, you're up first. Destination: Garr."

The huge rock alien smashed his boulder-like fists together. "G-Watch is over!" he bellowed.

"Wugrat, give that thing to me," Kaos said, reaching down to the rat and snatching the navicom transporter disk from its mouth. "Have you set it for Garr?"

The wugrat squeaked again and Kaos twisted the crystal's outer edge like a dial. He reached up and fastened it to Rockhead's arm. The navicom began flashing.

"Go get them," Kaos said to the invader.

Rockhead stomped to the centre of the cargo hold. *"Destroy!"*

The roof of the cargo hold opened, and Rockhead looked up at the swirling stars of the vortex. A blue light began to glow from the navicom and with a *whoosh* Rockhead shot out of the battleship and vanished into space.

CHAPTER
SIX

QUANTUM MUTATION SUIT

Back at G-Watch headquarters, Cosmo's
mind boggled from everything that the
G-Watch chief was telling him.

G1 stepped to the tinted-glass cabinet.
"I have something to show you, Cosmo."
He opened it and took out a spacesuit.
"This spacesuit is G-Watch's most
advanced piece of technology. It's called
the Quantum Mutation Suit and has been
designed especially for you. It's a body

armour for extreme combat." G1 handed it to Cosmo. "Try it on."

Body armour? Cosmo touched it. It didn't feel like body armour – it was flexible, like cloth. He held it up. It looked too big for him. "Er, I'm not sure this will fit me . . ."

G1 smiled. "We hadn't intended you to join us until you were a grown man."

"It should adjust," Nuri said encouragingly. "Try it on." She fetched him spaceboots, gloves and a helmet from the cabinet too.

Cosmo gingerly stepped into the spacesuit. He slipped his arms in, feeling small and foolish. Its sleeves hung down over his hands. He awkwardly pulled on the gloves, boots and helmet. All of a sudden the Quantum Mutation Suit began rippling. Cosmo could feel it moving over his skin as if it was alive.

"It's working, Chief!" Nuri said to G1.

G1 smiled. "You have nothing to fear, Cosmo."

Cosmo felt the suit tightening to fit him, moulding itself like a second skin. It started to glow electric blue.

"It's reacting to the power inside you, Cosmo," G1 said. "It's activating."

As G1 spoke, the helmet's visor lit up like a transparent computer screen in front of Cosmo's eyes. Words appeared: SYSTEMS CHECK STARTING. Lines of computer code raced across it.

"What's it doing now?" Cosmo asked.

"This helmet acts as a control module," Nuri said. She peered in at him through the visor. "It's just warming up. Some strange things should happen now, but you're perfectly safe."

The suit sparked as if lightning was running through it. Cosmo could feel it fusing with him, and his arms and legs tingled, hot one moment and cold the next. Suddenly his body started to change. Cosmo saw green reptilian scales appear on his torso, then on his arms, then on his legs. They were spreading over him – he was growing an alien skin!

He felt a little freaked out, but it didn't hurt – he just looked different. Then he felt the scales softening and gasped, seeing fine hairs sprouting through them. His skin was changing again into fur, thick black fur like a bear's. He took a deep breath and tried to stay calm.

"What's it doing to me?"

"Don't be alarmed, Cosmo," G1 reassured him. "It's just running through a few mutations."

Mutations? This is so weird! Cosmo thought. His body was changing before his very eyes. His furry skin transformed to prickly spines then to red feathers. *Feathers! How's this possible?* he wondered. Next his body turned sticky like slime, then red-hot like molten lava, then icy. It was incredible!

His hands and feet tingled – the gloves and boots were fusing too. They glowed brightly, changing shape. Cosmo now had long hooked talons where his feet should have been. His hands turned into large pincers and he snapped them together like a crab. He tried it again and they changed into paws. The next moment, his arms turned into long suckered tentacles. *Like a sea monster's!* Cosmo thought. He shook the tentacles and they changed into large leathery wings. *An alien dragon!* He beat the wings like he was flying.

On the visor, he saw more words appear: SYSTEMS CHECK COMPLETE. His wings receded, becoming arms again, and Cosmo returned to normal, dressed in the Quantum Mutation Suit. "How did it do all that?" he asked, dumbfounded.

"The Quantum Mutation Suit is made

from a fabric infused with particles from
the beginning of time when the universe
first came into existence," G1 explained.
"The same particles from which all life
came. Only you can activate it though,
with the power that you have inside you –
the power of the universe!"

"You can transform into any alien life

form you choose," Nuri said. "Just say 'SCAN' into the helmet's sensor to select your body type. It's voice-controlled."

"SCAN," Cosmo said, and on the visor's digital display, pictures of aliens appeared one after the other: winged aliens, underwater aliens, storm aliens . . . with details of their species, origins and features. The mutation suit was scrolling through its databank.

"It's 'MUTATE' to transform, and if you wish to return to normal just say 'RESET'. The sensors will still be embedded in your new form."

"I can really become any of these

aliens?" Cosmo asked. "This is amazing!" He lifted the visor on the helmet and looked at Nuri and G1 in astonishment.

"It's G-Watch's most formidable invention, a suit that will give you infinite capabilities," G1 told him. "Should you choose to accept your mission."

"The galaxy needs you, Cosmo," Nuri said. "Are you ready to fight?"

Suddenly Cosmo realized the seriousness of the situation. "And I'm the only person who can do this?"

"That's right," G1 said gravely.

Cosmo paused a moment. *There'll be extreme danger. I might not survive . . .*

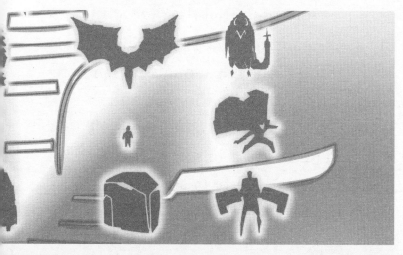

But inside him he felt an urge to say yes. "I'll do it!" he exclaimed.

G1 and Nuri both smiled.

"Splendid," G1 said, and he unclipped a handheld communicator from his belt. He spoke into it: "Surveillance, we're ready to go—" He paused as a voice replied. "Where's it heading?" G1 asked, his face clouded with concern. "Alert all agents! Mobilize the battle-droids! This is a RED ALERT."

G1 switched off his communicator, then turned to Cosmo and Nuri. "It appears that Kaos has navicom technology," he said. "Our interplanetary scanners have detected the first of the invaders beaming through the galaxy, and it's heading for our headquarters here on Garr." He approached the wall and touched his hand to a round sensor. The wall slid open and crimson daylight flooded into the secret headquarters.

Cosmo looked out over the mountains and heard a sound like thunder. He saw something enormous hurtling through the sky at phenomenal speed. It looked like a meteor. It came down between the mountains and struck the base of the canyon with a massive *boom*, sending up dust and rocks.

As the dust cleared, Cosmo gazed down and saw something emerging from a huge crater. It was a monstrous alien with a body of solid rock. It was ten times the size of an Earthling man and had fists like boulders. It stomped towards G-Watch headquarters, swinging a punch at the space cruiser on the landing strip. The cruiser spun end over end and crunched against the mountainside.

The monstrous alien looked up the mountain and roared, "I am Rockhead, and I have come to *destroy you*!"

CHAPTER SEVEN

MUTATE AND FIGHT!

"It's massive!" Cosmo said nervously. "How can I possibly fight that thing?"

Cosmo watched in horror as Rockhead lifted the crumpled space cruiser above his head. The massive rock alien hurled it at G-Watch headquarters, smashing it against the entrance. The mountain shook with the force of the blow.

"He's going to knock this place down, G1!" Nuri said.

Cosmo saw G-Watch battle-droids marching out from the main entrance, laser guns at the ready. There were a hundred of them – the entire platoon. They took up positions on the steps, ten rows of soldiers one behind the other, all pointing their lasers at Rockhead.

"In the name of the free galaxy, halt!" the droid commander shouted.

But instead Rockhead charged.

The battle-droids opened fire, shooting

at the invader, but their laser beams
bounced off him. Rockhead thundered up
the steps. He stamped on the first line of
droids, squashing them like tin cans.

G1 spoke into his communicator: "All
agents to battle stations!" He turned to

Cosmo. "It's time to fight," he said. "If you feel you are ready, meet us in the main hall." Then he vanished into thin air.

There was a loud *boom*. Cosmo looked down the mountainside and saw Rockhead charging at the huge stone doors. He'd swept aside the droid soldiers and was trying to force his way in. *He mustn't make it*, Cosmo thought.

"Come on Cosmo – downstairs!" Nuri called, zooming off on her hoverboard.

But Cosmo felt an energy welling inside him. *It's the power of the universe*, he thought. It was giving him courage.

"I'll see you at the bottom," he replied. He hopped onto his hoverboard and whizzed out of the opening in the top of the mountain. Cosmo made the board dip down, aiming it at Rockhead, then flicked down the visor on his helmet.

"SCAN," he said into the voice sensor. On the visor's digital display, images

of alien creatures appeared as the
Quantum Mutation Suit scrolled through
its databank: a two-headed vorpwolf, a
laser-eyed xarg, a fiery lavabear, a high-
voltage electrax . . . Cosmo compared
alien heights, weights and features.
Which alien can beat a living mountain?
he wondered. Then he spotted a huge,
muscular alien with a massive metal fist.

ALIEN: HAMMERFIST
SPECIES: OGRON
ORIGIN: PLANET AJAX
HEIGHT: 10.4 METRES
WEIGHT: 2.2 TONNES
FEATURE: IRON PUNCH

"MUTATE," Cosmo said into the
helmet's sensor. He felt his whole body
tingle; then he started to grow wider and
taller. His skeleton was re-forming itself,
his bones lengthening and thickening. It
was incredible! He was growing to over
ten metres tall, his skin stretching as

muscles bulged out all over his body. One
of his fists was enormous and made of
solid metal. He was Hammerfist!

The hoverboard sank under his massive
weight and he leaped down, landing by the
entrance with a thud. Around him, battle-
droids lay broken and twisted, but as
Hammerfist, Cosmo felt strong. He strode
past the mangled space cruiser towards

Rockhead, clenching his huge metal fist. "Hey, you. It's no entry!" he called.

Rockhead turned to face him. "No one can stop me!" the invader roared back, and he smashed his boulder-fists down, shaking the ground like an earthquake. He charged into Cosmo, driving him hard against the rockface. Cosmo felt his breath being knocked out of him. The invader's force was immense. "Prepare to be crushed!" Rockhead shouted.

Cosmo tried to push the rock alien off, but there was no way to budge him, even using Hammerfist's huge muscles. It was like wrestling with a living mountain!

Rockhead swung his boulder-fist, but Cosmo ducked just in time, and it smashed into the mountainside, sending rocks flying.

"You call that a fist?" Cosmo roared. "*This* is a fist!" He wrenched his metal fist free and slammed it hard against

Rockhead, sending sparks flying. The huge creature staggered backwards, stumbling over fallen battle-droids.

Cosmo threw another punch: this time his metal fist struck Rockhead's stomach. The alien doubled up under the force of the impact.

"You don't look so tough now, Rockhead. Is Hammerfist too powerful for you?"

As Hammerfist, Cosmo felt invincible. He swung his arm round in a circle, his metal fist gathering speed like a demolition ball. He landed a powerful uppercut to Rockhead's chin, and the alien's jaw cracked. "Give up, Rockhead, or Hammerfist will bust you!" Cosmo yelled.

But the blows only made Rockhead angrier. "Never!" he roared. He reached round, picked up the space cruiser by its cockpit and swung it at Cosmo. It

smashed into him, sending him tumbling down the steps, head over heels. He landed in a heap at the bottom.

"Hammerfist cannot stop me!" Rockhead bellowed.

Cosmo lay on the ground, battered and bruised from the fight. He could feel his energy waning, the power leaving him: Hammerfist's molecular pattern was breaking up. The Quantum Mutation Suit was failing. "RESET," he said, and Hammerfist's muscles began receding. Cosmo was shrinking, turning back into a boy.

Rockhead stared down at him from the top of the steps and laughed. "Ha! Ha! Haaaaaaaaaah! Look at yourself now. You are no match for me!"

Behind the alien, Cosmo saw the doors sliding apart. Six G-Watch battle-tanks trundled out from the mountain. They opened fire on Rockhead, blasting him with their sonic cannons.

The invader roared as the blasts hit, his craggy body shaking with the force of each impact. "That makes me mad!" he yelled.

Rockhead stomped to the lead tank and grabbed hold of its cannon. He lifted the tank off the ground and hurled it aside like a toy, then raised his fists, smashing them down on two more.

The huge doors slid closed again as the remaining tanks continued pummelling Rockhead with their sonic cannonfire.

"I shall let myself in another way," the fearsome alien roared. Rockhead stomped over the tanks and began to scale the sheer mountainside. He punched at the rock as he climbed – he was trying to force his way into G-Watch headquarters through the mountain itself!

CHAPTER EIGHT

"I WILL CRUSH YOU!"

Cosmo looked up in horror, seeing
Rockhead trying to smash his way into
G-Watch. Then he saw Nuri clambering
from the top of a mangled tank onto the
broken droids.

"Are you OK?" he called to her.

"We have to stop him, Cosmo!" Nuri
replied.

I need to climb up after him, Cosmo
thought, watching the invader on the

mountainside. "SCAN," he said into the helmet's voice sensor.

The Quantum Mutation Suit searched its databank, and once again, images of alien creatures scrolled down in front of Cosmo's eyes: a storm-eating torrnatron, a thousand-eyed telescopterix, an ice-breathing freezoth, a fanged wolverax . . . *What could climb?* He saw an image of a six-armed ape-like alien.

ALIEN: GRAPLAX
SPECIES: BURATANG
ORIGIN: PLANET ZOTH
HEIGHT: 7.6 METRES
WEIGHT: 1.2 TONNES
FEATURE: SIX LONG CLIMBING ARMS

Perfect, Cosmo thought. "MUTATE!"

He felt his body tingling as it changed, growing bigger and bigger, his skin turning to fur. He could feel his sides splitting and arms extending, six of them, each over five metres long, with ape-like hands. He beat his six fists against his chest. "Not so fast, Rockhead!" he called.

As Graplax, Cosmo ran like an ape, bounding along on his knuckles, taking the steps ten at a time. He vaulted over the broken droids and the wrecked tanks, then leaped up onto the sheer rockface.

"Go, Cosmo!" Nuri shouted. Cosmo looked down and saw her give him a thumbs-up then dash back into headquarters.

Cosmo gripped the mountainside with his six strong hands and began pulling himself up towards Rockhead, arm over arm.

The invader was already high up the mountain, smashing his fists against the rock, trying to find a weak spot where he could punch his way through. G-Watch headquarters was shaking. Boulders were dropping off the rockface like an avalanche, and cracks were beginning to appear in the mountainside.

All of a sudden the invader managed to punch his fist right through the rock, pushing his arm inside. Cosmo heard the screech of twisting metal and saw Rockhead pull out a bank of G-Watch control desks, throwing them down the mountainside. He saw agents tumbling down too, shooting grappling hooks from their utility belts to snag hold of the rockface and stop themselves falling.

"Hey, leave them alone!" Cosmo yelled.

Rockhead threw a bank of computers at him, trying to knock him off. But Cosmo swung across the face of the mountain, avoiding the debris. He grabbed hold of a rocky overhang.

"I will crush you!" Rockhead roared.

Cosmo pulled himself higher, clambering up in pursuit of the invader. Faster and faster he climbed, his six

arms working together. With one arm outstretched, he reached for the ledge beside Rockhead; then, with his other five hands, he tried to pull the enormous alien off the mountain.

"Graplax is taking you down, Rockhead!"

Cosmo wrenched one of his opponent's legs away from the rockface, then grabbed the other. Rockhead lost his footing, but had his arm pushed through the hole he'd punched in the mountain, stopping himself falling.

Cosmo and Rockhead were now locked together. Cosmo was pulling as hard as he could, but Rockhead was holding fast.

Just then, a section of the mountainside slid open, and Cosmo heard the roar of engines. Spaceships from the G-Watch battle-fleet flew out: starfighters, microjets and stealth drones.

While Cosmo wrestled with the alien,

trying to pull him off the mountainside, the spaceships circled Rockhead, blasting him with laser fire.

Rockhead swiped at a starfighter, swatting it and sending it spinning out of control. Its pilot managed to eject just in time, and the craft hit the ground, exploding on impact. Cosmo saw that the pilot was Nuri. She opened her parachute and floated down past him. "You can do it, Cosmo!" she called out to him.

But even as Graplax, Cosmo couldn't prise Rockhead off the mountain.

Rockhead shouted, "You won't stop me!" and once again smashed his fist into the rock. Cracks spread out and, suddenly, a chunk of the mountainside caved in.

Rockhead and Graplax both fell through the hole into the G-Watch surveillance room. Down they went, crashing through the levels, one after the

other, landing with a thud on the floor of the main cavern.

Cosmo felt shaken and battered, his power waning. "RESET," he said weakly. He felt his body tingling and he started shrinking, mutating back into a boy.

CHAPTER NINE

THE SWORD

Cosmo scrambled out of the way as
Rockhead rose to his feet. They were
inside G-Watch headquarters, standing
among the vehicles in the main cavern.
Laser guns were firing: G-Watch agents
were taking up positions and shooting at
the invader.

Rockhead laughed at Cosmo. "G-Watch
is finished! The galaxy is entering a new
age, the Age of Kaos!" He smashed his

fist down on the X1 Indestructible space plough, breaking it in two, then hurled a space buggy at the wall. G-Watch agents dived for cover as the fearsome alien pushed over the solar-powered rocket, sending it crashing to the floor.

"Hey, cut that out!" Cosmo yelled.

Rockhead turned and snarled, "Not given up yet, puny Earthling?"

The invader strode closer, his rocky

fists raised, ready to pulverize Cosmo.

One more try, Cosmo thought desperately. "SCAN," he said into his helmet's sensor. The Quantum Mutation Suit scanned through alien life forms, their images appearing on the visor's digital display. *How can I defeat Rockhead?* he wondered. An image of a jelly-like slime alien flashed across the visor, giving him an idea.

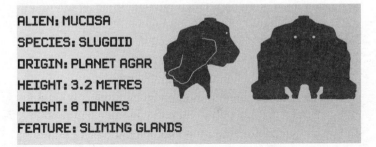

ALIEN: MUCOSA
SPECIES: SLUGOID
ORIGIN: PLANET AGAR
HEIGHT: 3.2 METRES
WEIGHT: 8 TONNES
FEATURE: SLIMING GLANDS

"MUTATE."

Cosmo felt himself changing once again, his body growing huge, squidgy and shapeless. It felt as if his skeleton had suddenly gone soft. Stalk eyes protruded from his huge jelly-like body, and slime started oozing from every pore.

As Mucosa, Cosmo faced Rockhead in the centre of the cavern.

The invader let out a roar of revulsion at the sight of his opponent. "Prepare to be squished, Slimeball!"

Cosmo held his ground, his stalk eyes spotting the rock alien clench his boulder-fists, ready to attack. Rockhead punched Cosmo with all his might . . . but Cosmo's wobbly body absorbed the power like jelly and he held his ground. The invader's fist sprang back, covered in slime.

Cosmo gurgled, "You can't hurt me, Rockhead."

The invader swung again, even harder. But again Cosmo absorbed the power of the blow, his blob-like body rippling. Rockhead punched with his other fist, but it was still no use. The invader's strength was useless against Mucosa. And with every punch Rockhead was getting covered in slime: thick, gooey slime that was slowing him down, making him heavy and sticky.

Cosmo oozed slime even more, leaking mucus from glands all over his body and even spewing goo from his mouth. He was attacking the invader with gallons of slugoid slime! Rockhead tried to throw a punch, but he slipped and slid, struggling to stay on his feet.

"I knew you'd come to a sticky end, Rockhead," Cosmo gurgled.

His mighty opponent roared with rage and swung his fist again, but lost his balance and toppled over. He tried to get up, but couldn't get a grip on the slippery floor. "You slimeball!" he shouted in fury.

Mucosa had done his work and the invader was down, but the slugoid had no way of dispatching him.

"RESET," Cosmo said, and his jelly-like body tingled as he turned back into a boy wearing the Quantum Mutation Suit. He looked at the G-Watch agents taking cover behind upturned and damaged vehicles. "Rockhead, you don't belong here," Cosmo said firmly.

Looking at the destruction around him, Cosmo felt his power surging, stronger than before, more physical this time, like electricity flowing through his veins. He could feel an invincible courage spreading through him, and the mutation suit glowed, sparking brightly. Suddenly, white and blue light burst from Cosmo's hand like lightning. He stared at it, shocked.

"It's your power, Cosmo," Nuri called. "Use it!"

The lightning-like energy was taking the form of a sword. Cosmo raised it and charged at Rockhead. "The power of the universe is in me!" he cried.

The alien roared as the power sword struck, "NO!" Then a look of hatred spread over his craggy features.

Cosmo could feel his power running through the sword into the invader. He felt defiant and strong, every molecule of his body vibrating, his power locked in battle with Rockhead's hatred. All at once cracks began spreading over the rock alien's body. Then, in an explosion of light, the invader vanished.

CHAPTER TEN

FOUR MORE TO COME

Cosmo stepped out of the pool of slime and heard the sound of applause. He looked round and saw Nuri and all the G-Watch agents clapping and cheering.

"Cosmo, you did it!" Nuri called.

G1 put his hand on Cosmo's shoulder. "You saved us, Cosmo. You've saved G-Watch," he said.

Cosmo wiped slime off his gloved hand. "The sword . . . where did that come from?" he asked.

"From inside you, Cosmo. It's a physical extension of your power – strong enough to destroy evil."

Cosmo took off his glove, but he couldn't see any trace of the sword now.

G1 smiled. "It will come again, Cosmo, when you next need it. Now that you have seen your power in action, you must decide whether to use it further and continue your mission. There are four more alien invaders set to attack: four more battles to fight. Are you willing to face them?"

Cosmo thought for a moment. *Four more invaders – this was going to be dangerous!* Back on Earth his mum would still be thinking he was on a galactic cruise.

But the galaxy needed him . . .

"I'll do it!" he said.

All the G-Watch agents in the cavern

cheered. "Way to go, Cosmo!"

G1 smiled, then picked up two hoverboards and handed one to Cosmo. "Follow me, I have a surprise for you," he told him.

They surfed up a level to the G-Watch spacefleet bay. Maintenance bots were already repairing the huge hole in the floor where Rockhead and Graplax had crashed through. The bay's takeoff hatch was open to the sky and mechanics were busy servicing the G-Watch battle-fleet after its fight with Rockhead. Amidst the dust and activity, Cosmo saw a group of G-Watch scientists standing proudly beside the Dragster 7000 spaceship – the ship was hovering off the ground, its thrusters throbbing.

"It's fuelled up and ready to go," one of them said.

G1 looked at Cosmo. "Hop in then. It's yours."

"My own spaceship!"

"Our finest," G1 said.

The ship lowered, and a door in its side slid open. Cosmo stepped in. It was brilliant: gleaming new and equipped with the latest technology. On the control desk a small bug-like robot bleeped.

"Welcome aboard, Master Cosmo," it said.

It was Brain-E, the little robot that had helped him land the cruiser. "G-Watch brainbot reporting for duty!" it said.

"Brain-E, are you coming as well?"

"If I may, Master Cosmo."

"Me too," said a voice behind Cosmo. He glanced round and saw Agent Nuri coming aboard. "If you'd like a co-pilot, that is," she grinned.

Cosmo laughed. "You bet. This is going to be a blast!"

He placed his helmet on the control desk and sat in the pilot's seat. Through the spacescreen he looked out at the crimson Garr sky. He could just make out Planet Mingus dipping behind the mountains.

He noticed G1 speaking into a handheld communicator, then a moment later the silver-eyed chief approached the Dragster's door. "Well, you'd better buckle up and set off," he said.

"Already, Chief?" Nuri asked.

"Our interplanetary scanners have just picked up a second invader beaming through the galaxy's Dyad-24 star system. We believe it to be the fire alien, Infernox. He is heading in the direction of the jungle planet Zaman, where many of the galaxy's medicines originate. It would appear that Kaos is targeting vital galactic resources."

"OK, G1, we're on to it," Cosmo said. He switched on the Dragster's thrusters. "Nuri, could you set the route to Zaman, please?"

"Yes, Captain."

Cosmo pressed a button, closing the ship's door, then released the docking clamps. He pulled the throttle and, with a blast, the Dragster 7000 shot out from G-Watch's secret headquarters, speeding him away on his mission.

"Infernox, we're coming to get you!"

ALIEN INVADERS

MAX SILVER

INFERNOX
THE FIRESTARTER

RED FOX

INVADER ALERT!

In the wild jungle of Planet Zaman, robot DEL-8 rolled between the trees on its caterpillar tracks, its forklift arms carrying a crate of sparkling berries. It trundled into a large clearing where Planet Zaman's only building stood – the Eco-Tec Medicines Laboratory. The delivery-bot swivelled its camera eye, blinking in the lilac sunlight, then rolled in through the laboratory door.

"Starberries for sorting," it announced through its voicebox.

Inside, hundreds more robots were at work, creating advanced galactic medicines from the plants that grew in the jungles of Zaman. Robot DEL-8 tipped the crate of starberries out onto a conveyor belt, where a team of sorting-bots began removing the berries' stalks with their pincers and cleaning them with electric brushes.

DEL-8 selected a tray of the juiciest berries and took them over to the processing area, where processor-bots were waiting, piston arms raised.

"Juicy starberries for pulping," DEL-8 said, placing the tray on a workbench.

The processor-bots squashed the berries to a pulp, then extractor-bots rolled in and sucked up the paste with their hoses, sending it into their mixing tanks. There was a whirr as they separated the chemicals, then squirted a sticky syrup into jars. The team of robots were preparing starberry syrup, one of the most precious medicines in the galaxy. It was the only cure for comet cough, a terrible illness carried in the toxic vapour trails of comets. Packager-bots packed the jars of syrup into boxes, ready to be collected by cargo ships and distributed to the galaxy's planets.

All through the laboratory, teams of robots were busy turning jungle plants into medicines: glimpan-tree wax for sun blisters, zinger-pollen spray for gravity sickness, mistlemoss cream for dongaloids, oozing-buckthorn ointment for tentacle tension, and even nut-nectar bug-eye drops.

Robot DEL-8 rolled out of the door to fetch another crate. But as it headed into the jungle, a loud roar sounded overhead. Its camera eye swivelled, glancing up through the trees. Its circuits whirred, puzzled by what it saw: a huge ball of fire was hurtling down through the sky.

DEL-8's processor calculated that the fireball was heading straight for the laboratory. It bleeped in alarm: "Danger! Danger!"

Suddenly the huge ball of fire smashed down onto the building. In a massive explosion, robots, machinery and medicines were blasted in all directions. DEL-8 was sent flying backwards, smashing into a tree trunk.

"Emergency!" it called, crashing to the ground. It tried to right itself, but its caterpillar tracks had jammed. Its camera eye focused on the burning laboratory. "Emergency!"

Flames raged through the building and thick black smoke rose high into the sky. Then out of the flames stepped an enormous alien creature.

DEL-8 bleeped fearfully, seeing the alien grinning. "Intruder! Intruder!"

The alien glowed red-hot and towered even higher than the burning laboratory. He roared menacingly, spewing fire from his mouth like a volcano.

"I am Infernox, and by order of Kaos I've come to set this planet ablaze!"

CHAPTER ONE

THE MISSION

"Destination: Planet Zaman!" Cosmo said, blasting the Dragster 7000 spaceship away from Garr. "Point me in the right direction, Nuri."

"Programming route co-ordinates now," his co-pilot, Agent Nuri, replied. She was tapping numbers into the spaceship's navigation console, a look of concentration on her blue-skinned face. "Done," she said. She tapped the spacescreen, activating its star plotter, and words lit up on the glass:

DESTINATION: PLANET ZAMAN
STAR SYSTEM: DYAD-24
ROUTE: HYPERWAY 55 FROM THE BIG DIPPER CONSTELLATION
DISTANCE: 2.6 BILLION MILES

Cosmo felt excited. Through the
spacescreen, in the distance, he could see
a pattern of seven stars shaped like a

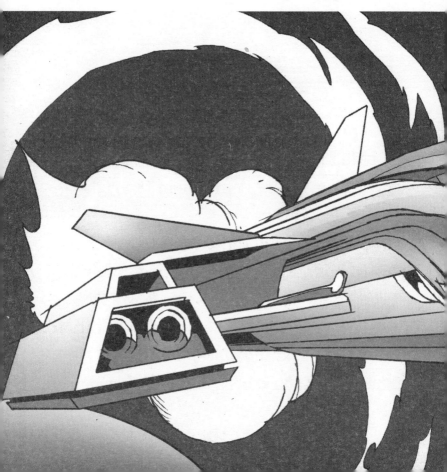

frying pan – the Big Dipper constellation.
"Are you ready for another adventure, Nuri?"

"I sure am, Cosmo!"

"Then it's full speed ahead!"

Cosmo nudged the steering column,
turning towards the Big Dipper, and
increased speed to eleven vectrons. They
were on their way.

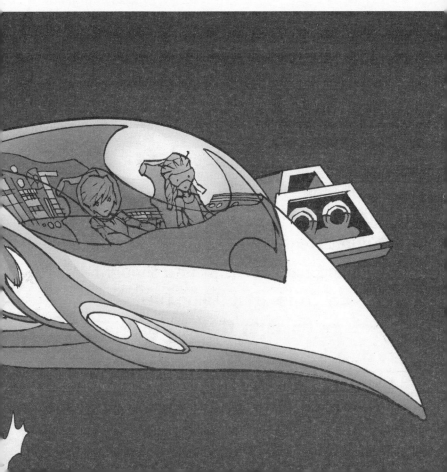

Cosmo Santos was an eleven-year-old Earthling boy on a mission for the galactic security force G-Watch to save the galaxy from five alien invaders. The invaders were being beamed in by the galactic outlaw Kaos, using navicom transportation devices, and were under orders to destroy the galaxy. So far, Cosmo had defeated the first of them – Rockhead, the living mountain – in a fierce battle on Garr. Now he was heading west to the jungle planet, Zaman, to face the second invader, the fire alien Infernox.

As he flew through space, he looked out in wonder, thinking what an amazing turn his life had taken. Only yesterday he'd left Heathrow Spaceport on Earth as a passenger on what he'd thought was a galaxy cruise. But it had turned out to be a secret plan by G-Watch to bring him to their headquarters on Garr, and from then on his whole life had changed.

Cosmo had discovered that he was unique. Inside him was a power – the power of the universe – which was present in all living things but unusually strong in Cosmo. It gave him courage and a lightning-like energy when facing danger. Cosmo's father had been the first to notice it in him when he was very young. Cosmo dipped the Dragster's fins, shooting through the stars of the Big Dipper. *If only you could see me now, Dad*, he thought. *I'm a G-Watch agent!* Cosmo's dad had been a G-Watch agent too, but had died two years ago in a space-crash. Cosmo still thought about him every single day.

Up ahead, the flashing lights of space beacons marked the entry to Hyperway 55, one of the galaxy's high-speed space lanes. Cosmo wove the Dragster between them then opened a panel on its steering column, revealing a silver switch.

"Engaging hyperdrive, Nuri," he said.

Cosmo flicked the switch and was thrust back into his seat by the force of the acceleration. The stars in the spacescreen turned to bright white streaks as the Dragster 7000 shot across the galaxy at hyperspeed, twice the speed of light.

"Are you ready to face the enemy, Cosmo?" Nuri asked.

"I think so," Cosmo replied, a little apprehensively.

"You can do it! Trust in your power, Cosmo," Nuri told him. "You'll be great – just like you were against Rockhead. And I'll be looking out for you too. We're a team, remember."

Cosmo remembered how he had beaten the first alien by transforming into Mucosa the slugoid. *Well, there's no turning back now*, he thought. As he blasted along the hyperway, a feeling of courage began to well up inside him, and his spacesuit glowed. He was wearing G-Watch's most advanced piece of technology – the Quantum Mutation Suit, a living body armour infused with particles from the beginning of the universe. Activated by the power inside him, it enabled Cosmo to mutate into alien forms to fight any opponent.

"We're nearly there," Nuri said. "Exit hyperway in seven seconds."

"Already?" Cosmo asked. "That was two-point-six billion miles? Wow, hyperspeed is fast!"

"... *four ... three ... two ... one ...*"

Cosmo flicked the hyperdrive switch back and turned the steering column. His ears popped as the spaceship veered off the hyperway then slowed to seven vectrons. Through the spacescreen he saw two enormous stars orbited by a cluster of vibrantly coloured planets.

"Welcome to the Dyad-24 star system," Nuri said. She tapped the screen, activating its star plotter, and words lit up on the glass beside each astral object.

PLANET UMAX ... PLANET OBON ... PLANET JUNOK ... PLANET ZAMAN! Cosmo read, seeing a large green planet straight ahead. He powered the Dragster towards it, slowing to two vectrons as they entered the planet's atmosphere. He switched the spaceship to planetary mode, and the cabin pressure self-adjusted as the ship flew into a lilac sky. Cosmo looked down and saw a vast jungle of trees veined with silver rivers. It was incredible – far bigger than any jungle on Earth. From his vantage point in the Dragster he could see the trees covering hills and valleys as far as the horizon.

"Zaman's jungle contains some of the most incredible plants in the universe," Nuri said. "It's where many of the galaxy's medicines originate from."

Cosmo took the Dragster low over the treetops to take a closer look. Some of the trees were enormous, and he saw alien creatures too: a herd of horned beasts grazing in a clearing; a flock of four-winged parrots flying alongside the Dragster. It was truly wild! He zigzagged along a winding river, then burst through the spray from a colossal waterfall.

Nuri checked the navigation console. "G-Watch's scanners plotted the invader's trajectory, and calculated that it would have struck around here. Keep an eye out."

Cosmo peered down apprehensively. *Where are you, Infernox?* he thought.

Nuri reached across the control desk and gently tapped a bug-like robot. "Brain-E, wake up – we've arrived."

Brain-E, the ship's brainbot, bleeped and

its lights came on. "Good day, Miss Nuri."

"I've never known a robot sleep as much as you do, Brain-E," Nuri laughed. "Tell us what you know about the alien invader Infernox."

The little robot stretched its six metal legs, then bleeped again, searching its databank. "According to my data, Infernox is an alien of volcanic origin from an ever-expanding sun in the Doom Vortex."

Cosmo gulped. He knew from his encounter with the first alien, Rockhead, how powerful aliens from the distant Doom Vortex could be.

"Infernox is a firestarter," the brainbot continued. "And can emit immense heat in the form of fireballs."

"Fireballs in a medicine jungle! That doesn't sound good!" Cosmo said. He peered over the trees and saw a column of smoke rising into the sky. "I think I've spotted where he struck. There's a fire over there!"

He looked down. Below, a building in a clearing was ablaze. Cosmo flew closer, looking anxiously to see if Infernox was still around, but thick black smoke was pouring into the sky and fierce flames raged thirty metres high. "I can't see properly. There's too much smoke," he said.

Nuri gasped. "The fire's out of control."

"We have to put it out before it spreads to the jungle," Cosmo told her.

Nuri went to check the kit shelves at the back of the cockpit. "We've only got a handheld flame-freezer, Cosmo," she said, grabbing a gun-like gadget. "It's designed for putting out engine fires, not huge fires like that. Those flames are too big!"

Cosmo banked the Dragster and circled above the burning building, desperately wondering what to do. The flames leaped around the spacescreen, the spaceship's engines making the air swirl violently.

"Careful, Cosmo," Nuri said. "You're pulling the flames towards us!"

That gave Cosmo an idea. *A crazy idea. But it might just work*, he thought. He pulled back the throttle, increasing the Dragster's speed. "Hold on tight, Nuri!"

"Cosmo, why are you accelerating?" she asked, alarmed.

"I'm going to make a whirlwind and try to suck these flames into the air," Cosmo replied, his heart racing. "I'm going to use the Dragster to put out the fire!"

CHAPTER TWO

A CRAZY PLAN

Cosmo fired the thrusters, sending the
Dragster 7000 around in circles above the
burning building. The speedometer crept
upwards – *two vectrons . . . three vectrons
. . . four vectrons* – the force pushing Cosmo
and Nuri back into their seats. Cosmo
tilted the Dragster on its side so that its
top touched the edge of the blaze.

"I feel dizzy, Cosmo," Nuri said, her
blue Etrusian skin tinged with green, as

if she was going to be sick.

"Me too!" said Brain-E. The little brainbot had clasped its legs around the navigation console on the control desk and was desperately trying to hang on.

The Dragster was making the air whirl round and round, drawing the smoke and flames into a spiral.

Cosmo accelerated even more. *Five vectrons . . . six vectrons . . .* He gripped the steering column tightly, making sure the Dragster didn't dip too low and crash into the jungle. The Dragster spun faster and faster, until Cosmo felt as if his stomach was rising up into his chest. He could hardly see through the spacescreen; it was a blur of smoke and fire and trees.

"Please slow down, Master Cosmo, my circuits aren't built for this," Brain-E called from the control desk.

The column of smoke and flames swirled faster, forming a burning whirlwind above the building. Cosmo steadily took the Dragster higher, circling faster still, and the flames rose with it. He was sucking the flames up out of the building, lifting them high into the sky.

"It's working!" Nuri said.

For a moment the fire raged, whirling in mid air. But with nothing to feed on, the flames began to die down, flickering and burning themselves out.

Cosmo eased off the throttle as the fire cleared, slowing the Dragster. His head was spinning. "Is everyone OK?" he asked.

Nuri had slid off her chair and Brain-E was dangling by one leg from the control desk. "My circuits feel peculiar," the brainbot spluttered.

Nuri pulled herself up, her face green but smiling. "Nice job, Cosmo!" she said.

Cosmo looked down, relieved to see that the fire was out, though the building was charred and black. "I can't see Infernox," he said. "Come on, let's go down and check the place out."

He reduced power to the Dragster's thrusters and descended, touching down beside the building on a scorched patch of ground. As he switched off the spaceship's engine, Nuri checked the external gauges.

"Temperature outside is thirty-six degrees centigrade," she said. "Gravity normal. Oxygen level plentiful."

Cosmo and Nuri both stood up and headed for the cockpit door. Cosmo pressed the exit release button and the door slid open. He felt warm air on his face and heard the hoots and caws of alien creatures coming from the jungle. He stepped down onto the burned ground, feeling a mixture of nerves and excitement; Zaman was only the second alien planet he'd visited.

"Master Cosmo, wait for me," Brain-E called, scuttling after him.

"Be careful, everyone," Nuri said. "Infernox could be nearby." She had the flame-freezer in one hand; with the other she took a phaser gun from her utility belt and held it ready in case the alien invader was waiting to ambush them.

Cosmo's heart was pounding as he crept towards the blackened shell of the building. "What is this place?" he whispered. "It's ruined."

Brain-E followed, picking its way carefully along the hot ground. "According to my databank, Master Cosmo, this was the Eco-Tec Medicines Laboratory," the brainbot said. "It's where galactic medicines are made."

The charred remains of dozens of robots lay on the ground, their circuit boards blown open and their casings melted. Brain-E went over to one and examined it. "Its circuits are frazzled."

Nuri leaned down to see. "Caused by an explosion," she whispered.

Cosmo cautiously stepped inside the burned-out laboratory, his spaceboots crunching on hot ash and broken glass. The laboratory's walls were torn open and blackened, conveyor belts lay twisted and broken, and more charred robots littered the floor. He went over to inspect a large black crater. "Look at this, Nuri."

She peered in. "It's an impact crater," she said. Then she glanced up: most of the roof had caved in. "Infernox definitely beamed down here. He must be huge!"

"So where is he now?" Cosmo said. He headed back outside and looked around into the jungle. Suddenly he heard a *blip-bloop* from under a tree, and saw an upturned robot with forklift arms trying to right itself. "Intruder," its voicebox said weakly. "Bot DEL-8 reporting emergency. Intruder! Intruder!"

Cosmo rushed over to the robot and knelt down beside it. "Are you OK?" He saw that its caterpillar tracks had melted and its control panel was sparking.

The robot tried to swivel its camera eye to look at Cosmo but the mechanism was jammed. "Intruder alert," it said weakly.

"Did you see the intruder?" Cosmo asked it.

"Affirmative," DEL-8 replied.

"Which way did he go?"

The robot raised a forklift arm, pointing into the jungle. "Intruder went north." But the effort was too much for it. There was a sizzling sound, and wisps of smoke rose from its control panel.

Cosmo heaved it upright, and battery acid leaked out.

"Systems faaaailinggg-g," the delivery-bot said, its voicebox melting. "Bot DEL-8 make no more deliveries noooooooow." The light in its camera eye went out.

"No!" Cosmo said desperately, inspecting DEL-8 for any trace of life. But its wires were severed and its circuit board was blown. *This little robot's shut down for good*, he thought sadly. He wiped the soot from its control panel, then glanced back at the laboratory. "Brain-E, Nuri, come here quickly."

They rushed over to join him.

"This one's only just shut down," Cosmo told them. "It saw Infernox. It said he went north into the jungle."

"But the jungle's massive," Nuri said. "He could have gone anywhere."

Brain-E examined the delivery-bot's circuitry, inserting a probe arm into its control panel and downloading the information from its databank. The little brainbot then projected a three-dimensional map of the jungle from its holographic imager. "Might this be of help, master?"

"Nice one, Brain-E," Cosmo said. A miniature jungle landscape shimmered in mid air, and he and Nuri scanned it for information. They saw the Eco-Tec Medicines Laboratory at its centre; further into the jungle dozens more locations marked where the medicinal plants grew.

"DEL-8 said Infernox went north,"

Cosmo said, tracing his finger northwards from the laboratory through the 3D jungle. He came to a golden tree marked GLIMPAN. "What's this?"

Nuri looked worried. "It's a glimpan tree," she said. "Glimpan-tree sap is the cure for sun blisters."

Cosmo frowned. "Then we'd better hurry before Infernox burns it down!"

TRACKING THE ALIEN

Cosmo set off into the jungle, with Nuri
and Brain-E close beside, heading north
towards the glimpan tree. Nuri held her
phaser gun at the ready, and Brain-E
scuttled along the leaf-littered ground, its
scanners on full alert for the invader.

Cosmo looked up in awe. The trees
towered above him, taller than any he'd
seen on Earth, their branches fanning out
like gigantic green umbrellas, with shafts

of sunlight dappling their leaves. He saw a troop of alien monkeys swinging from vines. They looked different to Earth monkeys, with bright green fur and tails with hands. The jungle plants looked alien too: blue-leafed ferns, fluorescent tree mosses, and toadstools taller than he was. Alien flowers floated in the air, and he could smell their scents: peppermint, vanilla and cola.

"This place is incredible," he said.

Nuri stopped to examine a tree trunk. "Infernox has definitely come this way, Cosmo. This bark is burned."

Cosmo glanced left and right, keeping a lookout for the alien invader. A tall purple flower leaned down, puffing pollen in his face, and he jumped, startled. "There sure are some weird plants here," he said.

Brain-E bleeped. "Planet Zaman has one of the most diverse ecosystems in the whole galaxy, Master Cosmo. It has excellent soil, no winters and over thirty

hours of sunlight each day. It also has maximum humidity. It's the perfect climate for plants to prosper."

"But not for G-Watch agents – right, Cosmo?" Nuri smiled, wiping condensation from her visor.

"Don't worry about me," Cosmo laughed. He'd once been trekking in the jungle with his dad back on Earth and could handle the heat and humidity. He picked up the pace, ducking under tall arching tree roots and bouncing over spongy mosses.

They passed toadstools that glowed like electric lamps, and parted a curtain of hanging purple vines. They pushed through a thicket of giant waggling finger ferns, then waded across a sparkling stream, Cosmo carrying Brain-E. Nuri stopped on the far bank, kneeling to examine huge gouges in the wet mud.

"Something large has been this way," she said. "These are footprints."

"Infernox?" Cosmo asked.

"Brain-E, could you identify these please?" Nuri said.

The brainbot hurried over the muddy ground, extending its scanner arm. Shining a little laserlight, it measured the size and shape of the footprints, then ran the information through its databank. Its lights flashed as it searched for a match.

"These are the hoofprints of hogohons, Miss Nuri," it said. "Grazing beasts that roam in herds." From its holographic imager, Brain-E projected a small hologram of a three-horned beast that looked a bit like a dinosaur.

"We passed over a herd of those in the Dragster on the way in," Cosmo commented. "Are they dangerous?"

"They're best avoided," Brain-E told him. "They can be very territorial."

"Well, we have to keep going," Nuri said, and she pushed on northwards through the jungle, towards the glimpan tree.

Cosmo glanced around, checking that no hogohons were lurking in the thick undergrowth. He ducked under an enormous spider's web, and his arm brushed a fern crawling with orange ants. "Brain-E, are there any other dangers on Zaman?" he asked.

The brainbot's lights flashed and it projected a hologram of a thin yellow snake with two heads. "The most dangerous creature on Zaman is the twin-snake, Master Cosmo: a two-headed tree snake with powerful venom. Unless you have the antidote, one bite is fatal within twenty minutes."

Cosmo gulped nervously, carefully checking the trees for snakes. "So what's the antidote, Brain-E?"

"Yellowbell pollen," Brain-E replied.

Nuri glanced back. "Stay vigilant, you two, and keep up."

Cosmo clambered down a bank of gum palms, ducking beneath their low-hanging branches, then dashed through a swarm of buzzing yellow flies.

"Master Cosmo, I don't wish to alarm you," Brain-E said, "but my sensors are detecting smoke ahead of us."

Uh-oh, Cosmo thought. He sprinted past Nuri. "Nuri, hurry!"

As a breeze blew through the trees, Cosmo smelled the smoke himself. He heard the crackling of fire and ran into a clearing where a tall golden-leafed tree was ablaze. "It's the glimpan tree! We're too late, Nuri! Infernox has already been here!"

Nuri rushed to Cosmo's side and pointed the flame-freezer towards the flames. She pulled its trigger, sending out freezing cold pulses. The fire hissed and sputtered.

On the ground around the tree Cosmo saw more charred and frazzled robots. He rushed to see if any were still moving,

raising his hands to shield his face from the blaze.

"They're harvester-bots, Master Cosmo," Brain-E said, checking their circuit boards. "They care for the jungle plants."

They had heli-packs for flying, pincers for picking fruit, and hoses for watering, but all lay broken and burned.

Suddenly Cosmo heard a hooting cry from the glimpan tree. He looked up and saw a creature clinging to a branch, trying to escape the flames. It was about the size of a koala, but pink and slimy.

"Brain-E, there's an animal up there!" he cried.

Brain-E raised a telescopic eye. "It's a tree sloth, Master Cosmo. A young one. The poor thing is trapped."

"Then we've got to save it!"

CHAPTER FOUR

HELI-PACK RESCUE

Cosmo looked up at the helpless tree sloth, trying to think of a way to rescue it. *If I use the Quantum Mutation Suit, I could turn into a flying alien and fly up there*, he thought. He called to Nuri, who was still fighting the blaze with the flame-freezer. "Nuri, I'm going to mutate to save the tree sloth."

"No, Cosmo!" she shouted. "Mutating now will deplete your power. You need to save your strength for Infernox. I'll get these flames under control."

But the blaze was now burning even more intensely and was about to reach the tree sloth. Cosmo could hear it hooting for help. Thinking quickly, he reached down and began detaching the heli-pack from one of the burned-out harvester-bots. "Brain-E, do you think you can get this working again?" he asked.

"I should think so, Master Cosmo," the little brainbot said. It inserted two pincer arms into the heli-pack's control panel and touched two wires together. There was a spark, then its rotor blades began spinning. "Hold on tight," the brainbot said.

Cosmo held the heli-pack above his head. "Nuri, I'm going up," he called. "Keep battling the flames."

The rotor blades whirred, lifting Cosmo off the ground and carrying him up beyond the flames. He could feel the heat around him, and saw bubbling sap spitting from the tree's burning bark. He rose higher and reached out to the tree sloth. He gripped its slimy paw and it coiled its tail around his wrist.

"That's it. I'll get you out of here," Cosmo said.

"I'll clear you an exit route, Cosmo!" Nuri called.

Cosmo felt an icy blast and saw the flames subsiding around him, clearing the way down. The tree sloth was now safe in his grasp, but he didn't know how to get the heli-pack to take him down again.

"Hold on tight, little sloth!" He let go and dropped to the ground, landing in a heap as the heli-pack spun into the burning tree and exploded.

"Master Cosmo, are you OK?" Brain-E called, hurrying over.

Cosmo stood up, dusting himself down. The slimy tree sloth let go of his arm and hooted in gratitude. "I'm fine, Brain-E. The tree sloth is safe."

Brain-E extended a probe arm to check it, and the slimy sloth cuddled the little brainbot, covering it in pink slime. "Er . . . hello to you too," said Brain-E.

The sloth hooted once more, then, on all fours, padded slowly into the bushes.

Cosmo was glad that he'd saved the sloth, even if it was only one small creature. He glanced at Nuri, who was now bringing the blaze under control. "Will the glimpan tree survive?" he asked.

"Its bark is charred, and it's lost its leaves, but it will recover eventually," Nuri replied, sending out another blast from the flame-freezer, making sure the fire was completely extinguished. She clipped it onto her utility belt and wiped the sweat from her face.

Looking around at all the destruction – the blackened glimpan tree and the frazzled harvester-bots on the ground – Cosmo felt angry; his power welled up inside him. "We have to stop Infernox – fast," he said determinedly. "Before he destroys any more medicinal plants on the planet. Map please, Brain-E."

The brainbot switched on its holographic imager and projected the map of the jungle into the air.

Cosmo studied it. *Which way now?* he wondered. He saw all kinds of medicinal plantations to the northeast: a mistlemoss glade, rednut trees, ghostfungus, buckthorn bushes, and a grove of starberry trees along a riverbank.

Nuri looked at the map and gasped. "Oh my goodness, starberry trees!" she said. "If Infernox destroys those, thousands of galactic citizens will die – starberry syrup is the only cure for comet cough."

"Comet cough?"

"It's lethal, Cosmo. I had comet cough when I was little and nearly died. Starberry syrup is what saved me."

"Then we have to hurry," Cosmo said.

Nuri tapped a switch on her visor and it turned a dim red colour. "We'll use my visor's thermal imager to help detect him," she said, and they raced off through the trees.

CHAPTER
FIVE

STAMPEDE

Far across the galaxy at G-Watch headquarters on Garr, G1 – the Chief of Galactic Security – paced to and fro in the surveillance room. All satellite feeds were down and no signals were coming in from the Dyad-24 star system.

A bearlike alien, Agent Toki, was operating the satellite switchboard with his hairy clawed paw. "There's some kind of jammer in operation, Chief."

"A jammer? It must be *him*," G1 replied.

At that moment the surveillance room's video wall flickered, and he saw an image of the five-headed alien, Kaos.

"It's no use, G1, I've blocked your signals," Kaos sneered. "I'm just saying hello, should you wish to surrender."

"Get off this frequency, Kaos," G1 said.

Kaos's five heads grinned, then his five noses twitched. "Oh dear, G1, I smell smoke in your galaxy. Oh yes, that's right – that crazed firestarter Infernox is carrying out my orders to destroy Zaman. Ha! You *LOSE*!"

G1 glared at Kaos with his silver eyes. "Withdraw the invader, Kaos."

"Now why would I want to do that?" Kaos asked him. "Infernox will soon burn all Zaman's precious medicines, and sickness and disease will spread throughout your galaxy. There will be plagues of gravity ulcers, solar boils

164

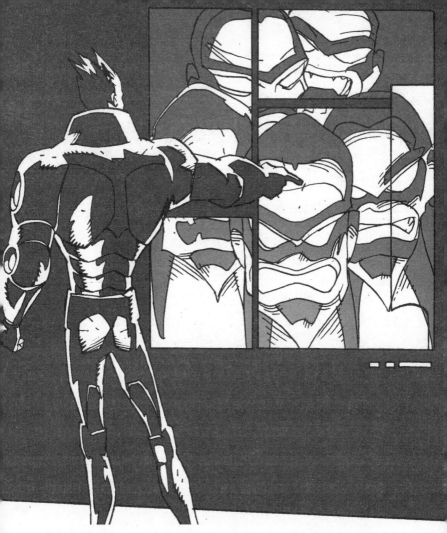

and moon measles – not to mention fatal comet cough. What will you do without your jungle medicines, G1? Billions will suffer and die, and the galaxy will beg me for mercy."

"Your invader will be stopped, Kaos,"
G1 said defiantly.

"Infernox will incinerate anyone
who gets in his way." Kaos's five heads
laughed, then the video wall flickered
and went blank.

"The signal's gone, Chief," Agent Toki
called from the switchboard.

G1 turned to look at him. "Get the
satellite feeds back up as quickly as
you can."

"Do you think the boy will be OK, Chief?"

"If anyone can defeat Infernox, the
Earthling can," G1 replied. "The power of
the universe is strong in him."

***

On Planet Zaman, Nuri led the way
northeast through the jungle, Cosmo
and Brain-E following close behind. With
her visor's thermal imager she could see
the heat trail that Infernox had left.

Cosmo noticed frazzled ferns and blackened bushes. He saw scorch marks on a fungi-ladder tree, the mushrooms on its trunk crispy and cooked. As they picked up the pace, scrambling their way through the jungle, he began to feel a little apprehensive. "Nuri, Infernox seems really powerful," he said.

"You can beat him, Cosmo," Nuri replied. "Trust in your power." She stopped beside a bush of orange berries. "Here – have one of these," she said. "You need to keep your strength up." She picked a berry and handed it to him. "These are multiberries. They grow on my home planet, Etrusia, too."

Cosmo suddenly realized how hungry he was. He hadn't eaten anything since his flight from Earth the day before! He chewed the multiberry and tasted all kinds of flavours: coconut . . . banana . . . strawberry . . . sausages . . .

Sausages? Cosmo thought. *Weird!* He kept chewing, and tasted chocolate, then apple pie.

Brain-E bleeped from beside the bush. "Multiberries contain all the goodness of a meal, Master Cosmo."

Cosmo could feel himself getting stronger. His courage was returning, and he leaped across a stream, determined to do his very best to defeat the invader.

Suddenly Nuri's pointy ears twitched. "I can hear something," she said.

"What is it?" Cosmo asked. Nuri's Etrusian hearing was superior to his own.

"I don't know. But there's something coming our way!"

Just then Cosmo felt the ground tremble. He heard roaring and rumbling, then branches snapping and birds squawking as they flew out of their nests up into the sky. He saw a curtain of vines part and a herd of large dinosaur-like creatures come charging through, heading straight for him and Nuri.

"Hogohons!" Nuri cried.

Brain-E leaped onto her arm, wrapping its legs around her like a wristwatch. "It's a stampede! Run!"

Cosmo and Nuri raced through a thicket of fangtail ferns, the hogohons charging behind, snorting and roaring.

"Faster – or we'll be trampled!" Nuri yelled, sweeping aside thorny leaves.

They sprinted down a slope, slipping and sliding on clumps of mucous moss. Cosmo glanced over his shoulder and saw the hogohons gaining, their hooves pounding like thunder.

"Why are they stampeding?" he yelled.

"Something must have spooked them," Nuri replied. "Just keep running!"

They raced into a grove of fungi-ladder trees, and Cosmo saw monkeys overhead, swinging through the branches,

screeching in panic. Parrots cawed and flew up out of the trees. All the jungle animals were in a frenzy.

The hogohon herd had almost caught up with them. "Up, Nuri!" Cosmo said, leaping into a fungi-ladder tree, using the mushrooms on its trunk as steps. Nuri raced up behind him, and they clung to a branch as the beasts charged past below.

"That was close," Nuri said, breathing heavily.

"Way too close," Cosmo agreed. He heard a whirring sound above his head and looked up, seeing harvester-bots buzzing upwards on their rotor-blades, fleeing the jungle.

Cosmo climbed higher so he could better see what was happening. The tree swayed as he pulled himself up from branch to branch. He must have been more than forty metres from the ground when he pushed his head out above the canopy and gazed around. To the northeast he saw

smoke billowing into the sky. "Fires, Nuri!"
he called. "The jungle creatures are
spooked because there are fires." He
counted twelve separate blazes. "Infernox
has gone on a rampage!"

Nuri climbed up through the leaves with

Brain-E on her wrist, and saw fires and
smoke everywhere. "We'll never put all
those out with the flame-freezer," she said.

Cosmo took a deep breath. *If we don't
stop Infernox soon*, he realized, *the entire
jungle will burn.*

CHAPTER SIX

A NASTY BITE

Cosmo and Nuri watched the harvester-
bots whizzing up from the trees around
them, trying to escape the blaze.

Brain-E bleeped to one and it stopped,
hovering in mid air alongside them.
Brain-E spoke to it in some kind of robot
language, then sprang off Nuri's wrist into
the air and took hold of the harvester-bot's
picker arm; together they flew off.

"Where are you going?" Nuri called.

"You two get Infernox. Leave the jungle fires to me!" the brainbot called back.

Cosmo scanned the jungle looking for the invader, and to the northeast saw fresh flames raging as another fire took hold. "Nuri, one over there just started. Infernox must be that way."

"Oh no! Then he's nearly at the river where the starberry trees grow!"

Suddenly they heard a hideous roar that sent shivers down their spines.

"Let's go!" Cosmo cried.

They started scrambling back down the tree. "We'll travel monkey-style," Cosmo said, reaching for a vine. "It'll be faster." He gripped hold of the vine and swung on it.

"Good idea, Cosmo," Nuri called, following him.

Cosmo leaped from vine to vine through the jungle like a monkey, heading for the river and the starberry trees. Leaves

brushed against him and smoke clouded his visor as he approached a grove of burning balloon bushes. He spoke to Nuri via his helmet's communicator: "If we want to stop Infernox, we're going to have to take the heat, Nuri. Swing fast!"

They raced over the top of the burning balloon-shaped plants, fire licking at their ankles. Cosmo's foot brushed one, and it exploded in a shower of red embers. Nuri blasted her flame-freezer downwards, trying to quench the flames.

Cosmo could barely see for smoke, but he could just make out the sound of the river up ahead. "We're getting close, Nuri!"

But as they emerged from the smoke, Cosmo suddenly felt a stinging pain in his shoulder. "Aaargh!" The pain shot through his body and he fell from the vine onto the jungle floor.

Wrapped around his arm was a yellow

snake with two heads. *A twin-snake!*
Cosmo saw fang holes in the shoulder of
the Quantum Mutation Suit. The snake
had bitten him! He shook it off and
shuddered with pain.

"Cosmo, what happened?" Nuri called,
jumping down beside him. She saw him
clutching his shoulder, and the snake

slithering away. She gasped, realizing the seriousness of the situation.

"It must have slithered onto me when I was swinging through the trees," Cosmo told her. He glanced at his shoulder. The fang holes in the suit were healing over, the suit's living mesh repairing itself, but it was too late: the snake's venom was already coursing through his veins.

"You need the antidote, Cosmo. Yellowbell pollen. Or you'll die."

Cosmo remembered what Brain-E had told him: that the bite of a twin-snake would bring about death within twenty minutes. "I know. But there isn't time to search for yellowbells," he said. "I have to fight Infernox now and save those starberry trees, or thousands of galactic citizens will die too."

"Then *I'll* look," Nuri said.

Cosmo raced off into the trees, trying to put the pain and fear from his mind.

He burst through the bushes onto the riverbank, where a row of shining starberry trees grew at the water's edge. And striding towards them was the enormous alien, Infernox.

The invader was over ten metres tall, with flaming red muscles that bulged and glowed, veined with molten lava. He was rolling a huge ball of fire in his hands, and the ground sizzled beneath his red-hot magma feet. He hurled the fireball at a starberry tree, making it burst into flames.

"Hey, leave those trees alone!" Cosmo shouted, sounding braver than he felt.

Infernox turned and saw him. "And who are you?" he roared.

"Cosmo Santos, G-Watch agent."

The alien laughed. "Ha! I will fry you!"

He hurled a fireball towards Cosmo – who leaped out of the way as it exploded behind him.

It was time to use the Quantum Mutation Suit. "SCAN," Cosmo said into his helmet's voice sensor. Images of aliens appeared on the visor's digital display as the Quantum Mutation Suit searched through its databank: an iron-shelled anvilon, a ten-clawed cortarg, a supersonic storm-hawk . . . Cosmo assessed their heights, weights and abilities. *Which could beat a firestarter?* he wondered. On the display appeared an image of a ferocious bear-like creature with a glowing hot body:

ALIEN: MAGMUS
SPECIES: LAVABEAR
ORIGIN: PLANET VULCANA
HEIGHT: 7.4 METRES
WEIGHT: 5.2 TONNES
FEATURE: VOLCANIC STRENGTH

Magmus the lavabear it is, Cosmo decided. He spoke into the helmet's voice sensor: "MUTATE!"

CHAPTER SEVEN

TIME TO TRANSFORM

Cosmo felt his body tingle as the energy inside him activated the Quantum Mutation Suit. The tingling grew stronger, like electricity flowing through his veins. The mutation suit was fusing with the molecules of his body. He could feel his cells re-forming as his body grew larger and more muscular. His hands and feet turned into massive clawed paws and his jaw lengthened, filling with sharp teeth.

He felt himself heating up, glowing red-hot like volcanic lava. He was Magmus the lavabear!

He padded towards the invader and snarled, "Prepare to be extinguished, Infernox!"

Seeing him, Infernox took a step back. "What magic is this?" he said.

Cosmo felt strong. As Magmus, he scraped the ground with his paw, and with a burst of explosive power charged at Infernox. He shunted the red-hot invader backwards, tumbling him head over heels. As a lavabear, Cosmo was resistant to the heat. Infernox rose to his feet, but Cosmo swung his volcanic glowing paw and struck him hard on the chin.

Red-hot sparks flew from the invader's molten face and he roared with anger: "No one fights Infernox and lives!"

But Cosmo felt no fear. He took hold of Infernox, pinning his arms to his sides in a crushing bear hug. He squeezed tighter and tighter. A furnace was raging inside him, building pressure like a volcano. "Give up, Infernox!" he roared.

"Never!" the alien snarled. "I come on the orders of Kaos to destroy this planet!"

Cosmo held on with all his might, squeezing the invader, but his left arm and shoulder felt suddenly shaky – the venom from the twin-snake bite was starting to take effect. A wave of weakness washed over him and he felt his bear-strength failing. Suddenly flames blasted out of Infernox's body, hurling Cosmo backwards onto the ground.

"RESET," Cosmo said, and his lavabear body tingled as he turned back into a boy wearing the Quantum Mutation Suit. *I need that antidote fast*, he thought. He looked around for Nuri, but couldn't see her anywhere. "Nuri, where are you?" he said into his helmet's communicator.

"I'm still searching, Cosmo," came a crackly reply in his earpiece, as if she was almost out of range. "No sign of any yellowbells yet. Are you OK?"

But Cosmo didn't get a chance to reply. Infernox was striding towards him.

"I will destroy you and torch this planet!" the alien roared.

Cosmo staggered to his feet, weak from the venom but determined not to give up. "Oh no you won't!"

He summoned what strength he had left and shouted, "SCAN!" into the helmet's sensor. The Quantum Mutation Suit responded instantly. Images of aliens appeared on the visor's digital display: a sabre-toothed skreen-bird, a viper-headed whalax, a toxic tumon . . . He saw an image of a large lizard-like creature with scaly skin and a tail like a whip.

ALIEN: CHAMELAX
SPECIES: REPTILION
ORIGIN: PLANET KLOSS
LENGTH: 12.4 METRES
WEIGHT: 3.3 TONNES
FEATURE: ALL-TERRAIN CAMOUFLAGE

Camouflage will give me the advantage of surprise, Cosmo thought. *Chamelax it is.* "MUTATE!"

He felt his body tingling as its molecules began to mutate. He dropped onto all fours, growing bigger, with four muscular legs and a long whiptail. Scales covered his body – thick, tough scales like armour. He padded towards Infernox and they changed colour, to shades of green and yellow, camouflaging him against the bushes. He crawled stealthily along the river's edge.

"Furnace Face, over here," Cosmo hissed, a lizard's tongue flicking from his mouth.

Infernox was rolling a huge ball of fire. "Where did you vanish to?" he demanded, looking around.

Cosmo crept up behind him, his reptilion scales flashing with silver, camouflaging him among the sparkling starberry trees. As Chamelax, he blended with his surroundings perfectly. "I'm right behind you," he hissed. He swung his whiptail as fast as he could, lashing the invader hard.

Infernox roared with fury: "Argh!" He spun round, confused. "Show yourself!"

Cosmo whipped him again. "Can't you see me? Ha!" He ran round the invader as Infernox blasted flames off target. Cosmo lifted his tail high, ready to strike again, but suddenly it felt heavy, too heavy to swing – the venom from the twin-snake was weakening him again. Cosmo felt his strength leaving, the power inside him failing as the venom took hold. Chamelax's camouflage began to fade.

Infernox turned, glaring at him. "I see you now!"

The mighty fire alien shot a torrent of flames straight at Cosmo, blasting him back along the riverbank.

Cosmo's reptilion skin flashed different colours in the heat, then his whole body convulsed. The effects of the venom were worsening – Cosmo couldn't fight back.

"RESET!" he said, transforming himself back into a boy.

"There's no escape!" Infernox roared, hurling a fireball as Cosmo dived into the river for safety.

He ducked under the water, swimming to the bottom as another fireball exploded on the water's surface in a flash of orange. Looking up through his visor, he saw the looming flame-red figure of the invader staring down from the riverbank.

Now what? Cosmo thought desperately.

The Quantum Mutation Suit was watertight but there was only a small amount of air in his helmet – it wouldn't last long. He felt his power draining away, as the venom in his bloodstream sent pain searing through his body. He could see the invader rolling another fireball. *I can't let Infernox win*, he thought. *The galaxy is relying on me. I have to fight. I have to!*

CHAPTER EIGHT

OVER THE EDGE

"SCAN," Cosmo said into the sensor of the Quantum Mutation Suit. On the visor of his helmet, images of aliens appeared once more.

My advantage is in staying underwater, he thought. *The fire alien clearly doesn't want to come in.* He had an idea, and selected an enormous underwater alien with ten long, gripping tentacles.

ALIEN: DECAGORG
SPECIES: MEGA-SQUID
ORIGIN: PLANET SEAMAR
LENGTH: 13.2 METRES
WEIGHT: 7.3 TONNES
FEATURE: GRAPPLING TENTACLES

Cosmo summoned the last of his strength and yelled, "MUTATE!"

He felt a tingling again as the molecules in his body transformed. His body was becoming flexible. Ten long suckered tentacles pushed out of his sides, each as thick as a tree trunk. His flesh became see-through like a jellyfish, and feathery gills formed on his neck, enabling him to breathe underwater.

As Decagorg, Cosmo stealthily edged towards the riverbank where Infernox was standing. He saw the starberry trees burning beside the firestarter. Stretching out his tentacles, Cosmo pulled himself along the river bed, his huge body rippling in the current. His eyes were now on the top of his head, and he could see the invader standing above him. Infernox's body was pulsing red and yellow, flames blazing from within.

"Are you hiding? Give up, do you? Ha ha ha!" Cosmo heard him roar. Infernox was laughing as though he'd already won.

Cosmo took a deep breath, his gills hungrily drinking in the water around him. Suddenly, from under the water, he shot up two long tentacles and grabbed hold of the invader's legs. His wet suckers steamed from Infernox's heat, but he didn't let go. Using all his mega-squid strength, Cosmo yanked hard, and Infernox splashed

into the water with a mighty hiss of steam.

"*Aargh!*" the invader roared.

The river bubbled, glowing fiery red.
Cosmo wrapped his tentacles around
Infernox, holding him down under the
water, trying to extinguish his flames.
The invader was struggling frantically,
his red-hot body sending up clouds of
steam. The water boiled as the two
mighty aliens battled for supremacy.
As they grappled underwater, they were

being washed downstream by the
current, faster and faster, bumping and
scraping over boulders on the river bed.

I have to keep the fire alien submerged,
Cosmo thought. But the venom was
numbing his tentacles. The invader
prised them off one by one, breaking free,
and surged to the surface.

"I shall prevail!" Infernox roared.

All of a sudden, Cosmo heard a rumbling sound from up ahead. It was growing louder, and the air above the river was filling with spray. They were approaching a waterfall! Cosmo braced himself then, summoning all his power, grabbed hold of Infernox's leg and dragged him over the edge.

Down they fell, tumbling in a mass of tentacles and steam. With an almighty splash, they plunged into a lake below and were driven under by the weight of the water crashing on top of them. In the churning current Cosmo lost his grip on Infernox, rolling over and over before rising back up to the surface. The force of the current spat him out like a giant cork and, exhausted, he washed up in the lake's muddy shallows. Infernox appeared nearby, his massive body wrinkled and black, his fire almost out.

Cosmo tried to pull himself towards

the invader with his tentacles, but he had lost almost all his strength now. The struggle and the venom of the twin-snake were too much for him. Decagorg's tentacles were too heavy to lift.

Cosmo whispered, "RESET," and turned back into a boy wearing the Quantum Mutation Suit. His eyelids felt heavy, and images from his life flashed before him: places he'd been, things he'd done, his mother and father . . . His eyes closed – his life was slipping away.

But then, as if in a dream, a distant voice called to him: *Cosmo!* It was a voice he hadn't heard in a long time, the voice of his father. *Don't give up. The galaxy needs you. Use your power, Cosmo. Use your power.*

Deep within him, Cosmo felt a strength resisting his fate, a courage that wouldn't give in. He opened one eye and saw Infernox rising to his feet, now glowing a dull red and growing brighter every second. "I'm not finished yet!" the invader roared.

Neither am I! Cosmo thought, taking strength from his father's voice. With a supreme effort, he clambered to his feet, feeling the power flowing through him again. The Quantum Mutation Suit began to glow. *"The power of the universe is in me!"* he yelled.

A sword of white and blue light extended from Cosmo's gloved hand like lightning. He'd seen it only once before, when he'd defeated the first invader, Rockhead. It was the power sword, the power of the universe within him taking the form of a weapon.

"Time to leave the galaxy, Infernox," he ordered.

"Never!" Infernox bore down on Cosmo, fire burning in his eyes, about to blast him. Cosmo thrust the power sword upwards.

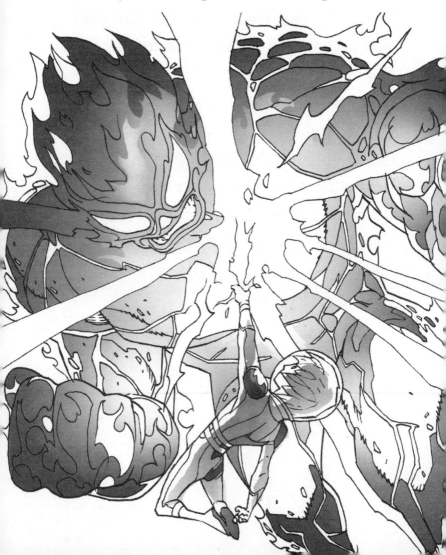

For a few moments his power and the invader's wrath were locked in battle. Every molecule in Cosmo's body was fighting for its life. He could feel power surging through him, extinguishing the invader's glow. Infernox roared and shook, convulsing and steaming. Then, all at once, he let out a cry of defeat: "*Aargh!*" His body hissed, and the alien evaporated into thin air.

"Good riddance, Infernox!" Cosmo said. He'd done it! He'd defeated the invader. He collapsed in a heap on the ground.

CHAPTER NINE

ROBOTS TO THE RESCUE!

"Cosmo! Cosmo, hold on!"

Through half-closed eyes, Cosmo saw Nuri clambering down vines beside the waterfall. She was calling to him, but he felt too weak to reply. She dropped to the ground and raced over, kneeling by his side.

"I did it, Nuri. I beat Infernox," he said weakly, but the venom from the twin-snake was now overpowering him, taking his life.

"I knew you'd win, Cosmo," she said.

Cosmo's vision was blurry. He could just make out Nuri holding a yellow bell-shaped flower.

"I found the antidote, Cosmo. It grows along the feeder streams upriver. I came as fast as I could." She gently opened Cosmo's mouth and shook the flower over it. Yellow pollen fell onto Cosmo's tongue. It fizzed, and after a few moments a warm strength began radiating through him. The antidote was working!

"You saved my life, Nuri!" he said.

"And you saved the galaxy from Infernox," she replied, smiling.

Cosmo sat up slowly, his strength returning, the venom nullified. "What about the other fires?" he asked.

Nuri pointed to Zaman's sky. Hundreds of harvester-bots were flying above the trees, sprinkling water from their hoses. "The harvester-bots are putting out the jungle fires. Brain-E gathered them all together."

Cosmo smiled. "Zaman's jungle and its medicinal plants are saved!"

He saw a harvester-bot coming down towards him with Brain-E dangling from it.

"Robots to the rescue!" the brainbot said, dropping to the ground beside him. "Master Cosmo, you beat Infernox. I knew you could do it!"

Cosmo blinked as Brain-E's lights flashed in celebration. "That invader won't be bothering the galaxy any more," he told it. "And Zaman will still be able to provide the galaxy with its vital medicines."

Nuri held out a helping hand to Cosmo. "Come on, let's get back to the Dragster," she said. "We'll radio G-Watch headquarters and tell G1 the good news."

Cosmo got to his feet, still feeling a little sore and light-headed, but now recovering from the fight and the effects of the venom.

Relieved to have succeeded in their mission, the trio headed off, triumphant.

* * *

Meanwhile, beyond the galaxy, in the cockpit of the battleship *Oblivion*, Kaos's five heads all stared at a blank monitor.

"What's happened to Infernox's navicom signal?" one head asked. "It was transmitting a moment ago."

"It's died! That's what's happened!" another head spat. "Infernox has failed."

"NOOOOO!" all the heads cried together. "He can't have!"

"He has!" hissed the first head.

Kaos marched up and down, his five heads muttering angrily. "So G-Watch has defeated the firestarter!" one head mumbled.

"And Zaman is saved – drat it!" another said bitterly. "What now?"

There was silence for a moment, then a little squeak came from the floor. The heads peered down and saw a purple rat licking its whiskers.

Kaos kicked it. "Well, don't just sit there, Wugrat!" he said. "Fetch me another navicom. It is time to unleash Zillah!"

All the heads cheered: "Zillah! Zillah! Zillah!"

Kaos hurried through the battleship to the cargo hold, where three huge aliens stood ready. "Step forward, Zillah," the outlaw said.

A huge fanged alien with spear-like limbs stepped from the group. "Zillah isss hungry," she hissed.

"Soon you shall feast to your heart's content," Kaos said, grinning. "Wugrat, hurry up!"

The purple rat scurried in carrying a crystal disc – a navicom transporter device. Kaos snatched it, turned its outer ring to set its coordinates, then reached up, attaching it to the alien. "Zillah, unleash

your terror," he said. "Destroy them!"

Zillah stalked into the centre of the hold on her long legs, then looked up as the roof slid open, revealing the swirling stars of the Doom Vortex. The navicom started to flash, and a blue light radiated from it. With a *whoosh*, Zillah shot up into space.

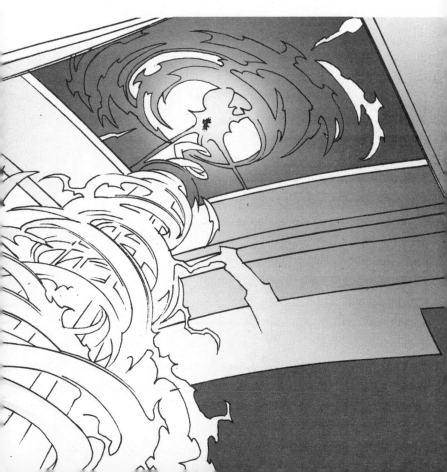

CHAPTER
TEN

DESTINATION: TRADEWAY

By the time Cosmo, Nuri and Brain-E
reached the Dragster, dusk was falling
over Zaman. Harvester-bots were
already busy rebuilding the laboratory.
Cosmo said goodbye to them and climbed
aboard the Dragster. He pressed a button
on the communications console and its
monitor flickered as it connected to
G-Watch headquarters. G1's face appeared
on the screen.

"Mission accomplished, G1," Cosmo said. "Infernox has been defeated."

The silver-eyed Chief of G-Watch smiled. "Congratulations, Cosmo," he said. "The galaxy is grateful to you. Its medicines are safe once again."

"Thanks, G1," Cosmo replied. "I couldn't have done it without Agent Nuri and Brain-E."

The brainbot flashed from the control desk and Nuri looked over from the co-pilot's seat, grinning. "Cosmo was ace, G1."

G1 looked at them gravely. "You have been exceptional, but your battles are not over yet. Our scanners have just detected a new invader beaming towards one of the galaxy's trade routes – the Great Western Tradeway. We believe it to be the fanged alien, Zillah – she must be stopped."

"We're on our way," Cosmo said.

"Good luck, team." The screen flickered as the transmission ended.

"Here we go again," Nuri said.

Cosmo started the Dragster's thrusters, then pulled back the throttle and blasted into the sky. He glanced down over Zaman's jungle – it seemed a happier place without the threat of Infernox: a herd of hogohons were grazing in a clearing again and a squadron of flying harvester-bots were waving goodbye.

Cosmo glanced at Nuri and smiled. "Set a course for the Great Western Tradeway. Let's go get Zillah!"

Join Cosmo on his next **ALIEN INVADERS**
mission. He must face – and defeat

ZILLAH
THE FANGED PREDATOR

INVADER ALERT!

Aboard space station *Orpheus*, Captain Provix kept watch as a convoy of eight cargo freighters approached along the Great Western Tradeway. The freighters were heading towards a vast zone of swirling asteroids: the Tarn Asteroid Belt. Provix reached out his webbed hand, switching on the space station's communicator. "*Orpheus* to convoy. I have a visual on you. Please reduce engine speed now."

"Instruction received," came the reply. "This is Convoy Leader Fortuna. How are conditions today? Are we in for a bumpy ride?"

Captain Provix pressed a sequence of buttons on the space station's control desk, activating its satellite receivers and deep-space imaging equipment. "The Tarn Asteroid Belt is experiencing erratic storms," he replied. "But *Orpheus* will guide you safely through. Sit back and relax. I'm locking on to you now."

The station's transmitters whirred as its supercomputer took control of the freighters' navigation consoles, overriding them and reprogramming their course.

Space station *Orpheus* was an advanced navigation station that monitored conditions in the Tarn Asteroid Belt, a wild zone of swirling rocks, debris and space dust that intersected the Great Western Tradeway. The area was a major danger to freighters trying to make essential galactic deliveries, and only *Orpheus* could guide them safely through.

Captain Provix had worked on *Orpheus* for six Tarn years. He was an experienced navigator from the distant planet Pialor, and his solitary temperament was well-suited to long periods spent alone in deep space. He watched from the control room as *Orpheus* remotely steered the eight freighters safely between moving asteroids, directing them on their journey through the Tarn Belt. He entered the convoy's details into the computer's log:

```
CONVOY: 10786956
COMPRISED OF: 8 DUCANOID FREIGHTERS
CARGO: GRAIN
DESTINATION: WESTERN WORL—
```

Suddenly the space station shuddered, throwing Captain Provix to the floor. *What was that – an asteroid hit?* he thought.

The emergency alarm sounded: *Whoop! Whoop! Whoop!*

Provix grabbed hold of the control desk, pulling himself up. Through the lookout sphere he saw *Orpheus*'s satellite dishes, antennae and probes spinning off into space. Warning lights were flashing on the control desk and the space station was rocking violently. Quickly he switched on the communicator. "Mayday! Mayday! This is Captain Provix requesting urgent help. Space station *Orpheus* is in trouble!"

He waited for a reply, but none came; the station's transmitters were down too. He heard a clawing and scratching sound coming from outside. *Something's attacking* Orpheus*!* he realized in terror.

Provix heard the station's metal hull being torn and wrenched apart. Suddenly there was a shrill hiss, and two long fangs pierced through the ceiling of the control room. Provix gasped. Green slime began oozing down the fangs, dripping onto the desk. It was some kind of chemical and the desk started to fizz and bubble, dissolving *Orpheus*'s supercomputer!

Captain Provix cowered, clinging to the control panel as the metal ceiling tore open and a hideous face looked in – the face of a huge fanged alien with jet-black eyes.

"I am ZZZZZillah," the alien hissed. "And in the name of Kaosss I come to feed!"

CHAPTER ONE

TRADEWAY TROUBLE

"Hey, Nuri, what are you doing back there?" Cosmo called, as he blasted the Dragster 7000 spaceship away from the Dyad-24 star system, heading for the galaxy's Great Western Tradeway.

Agent Nuri, his blue-skinned co-pilot from Planet Etrusia, entered through the cockpit's interior door. "I've brought you something to eat," she said, handing him a pot of pink paste.

Cosmo looked at it, puzzled. "What is it?"

"It's space food from the supply cupboard," she told him.

"It looks revolting," Cosmo said, wrinkling his nose.

Brain-E, the ship's brainbot, bleeped from the Dragster's control desk and dipped its probe arm into the paste. "Master Cosmo, this contains precisely two thousand calories, plus protein, minerals and vitamins A, B, C, D, E, K and P. It's been specially designed in the G-Watch laboratory for deep-space missions."

Cosmo scooped out a blob of the pink paste and swallowed it. "Mmmm, it's not bad," he said, surprised. It tasted like strawberry ice cream. He tucked in hungrily as the Dragster 7000 powered onwards, knowing he had to keep his strength up for what lay ahead.

Cosmo was an eleven-year-old Earthling boy on an urgent mission for the galaxy's security force, G-Watch. The evil outlaw, Kaos, had five fearsome alien invaders under his command, and was sending them to destroy the galaxy. Only Cosmo could protect it from their attack. Already he'd defeated two of them: Rockhead, the living mountain, and Infernox, the firestarter. Now he was trying to locate and fight the third invader: Zillah, the fanged predator.

"Nuri, could you select our course?" Cosmo asked.

"Right away," Nuri replied, programming the spaceship's navigation console. Details appeared on the spacescreen.

DESTINATION: GREAT WESTERN TRADEWAY,
TARN JUNCTION
STAR SYSTEM: TARN ASTEROID BELT
ROUTE: HYPERWAY 7 JOINING TRADEWAY AT JUNCTION L2
DISTANCE: 2 BILLION MILES

Having eaten, Cosmo felt ready for adventure. He'd been recruited secretly for this mission because of the unique power inside him – a lightning-like energy that gave him courage in the face of danger and activated the special spacesuit he was wearing, called the Quantum Mutation Suit. It was G-Watch's most advanced piece of technology, made from a living fabric that allowed Cosmo to mutate into different alien forms to fight any opponent.

He shot the Dragster between flashing space beacons onto Hyperway 7 then flicked the Dragster's hyperdrive switch; the stars on the spacescreen turned to bright streaks as he accelerated to twice the speed of light.

Nuri checked the course. "In two Earth minutes we'll reach Junction L2 of the Great Western Tradeway."

"What is this tradeway, anyway?" Cosmo asked.

"It's an essential route for spaceships travelling through the galaxy's Delta Quadrant," Nuri explained. "All kinds of freighters use it to trade supplies between the planets."

And now there's a fearsome alien on it, Cosmo thought. *Not good.* As they approached Junction L2, he switched out of hyperdrive and veered onto the Great Western Tradeway. He swerved to pass a slow-moving cargo ship then zipped by a line of livestock transporters. The tradeway was busy with space traffic; there were high-security ships transporting galactic gold and thick-hulled freighter vessels carrying food supplies.

Nuri glanced up from the navigation console. "G-Watch's scanners detected the invader beaming in near the Tarn Junction, where the tradeway enters the Tarn Asteroid Belt."

"Brain-E, what do you know about this invader?" Cosmo asked.

The ship's brainbot bleeped. "Well, according to my databank, Zillah is a female predator from the Doom Vortex; a scavenger who feeds on space wreckage in the vortex's treacherous storm zones."

"A scavenger that eats spaceships!" Cosmo said, shocked. "I don't want to end up as some freaky alien's lunch."

"Cosmo, slow down!" Nuri said.

Ahead of them was a space traffic jam: hundreds of ships were stuck on the tradeway. Cosmo reduced power. *What's going on?* he wondered. He weaved the Dragster between the ships, trying to find out. They were bottle-necked on the edge of a vast mass of swirling asteroids. On the spacescreen, the star plotter lit up, highlighting the asteroids, and a flashing red message appeared: DANGER! TARN ASTEROID BELT! DO NOT ENTER!

"This is weird," Nuri commented. "*Orpheus* should be guiding these ships through. There shouldn't be any jam."

"What's *Orpheus*?" Cosmo asked, flying carefully between two cargo carriers.

"It's a navigation station. It should be close by."

Cosmo peered nervously through the spacescreen sensing that something was wrong. "Nuri, over there!" he said, spotting a mangled silver structure floating on the edge of the asteroid belt. "Is that *Orpheus*?"

Nuri looked to where Cosmo was pointing. "Yes! What's happened to it?"

Cosmo steered towards the space station, shining the Dragster's searchlights. *Orpheus* looked broken and twisted. The bent remains of antennae and satellites were hanging off it.

"It's been attacked," Cosmo said. "Zillah must have struck already!"

The beam of the Dragster's searchlights illuminated someone floating in *Orpheus*'s control room – a wolf-headed man wearing an emergency oxygen mask.

"Look, someone's inside," Cosmo said. "And he's in trouble. He needs our help!"

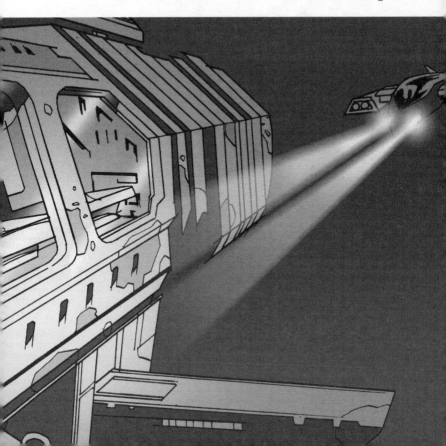

CHAPTER TWO

"IT'S BREAKING UP!"

Cosmo pulled up alongside *Orpheus*, attaching the Dragster to its docking magnets with a *clunk*. Pieces of metal were peeling off, drifting past the spacescreen.

"The space station's hull is breaking up. We'd better hurry," Nuri said, taking two white oxygen pills from her utility belt. "Swallow one of these, Cosmo. There'll be hardly any oxygen left inside."

Cosmo popped the pill into his mouth and felt it fizz. He grabbed a plasma torch from the kit shelf, then lifted the airlock hatch in the cockpit floor. "Brain-E, stay here and keep the engines running in case we need to make a quick getaway."

The brainbot flashed its lights. "Good luck!"

Cosmo stepped down through the hatch with Nuri following. She closed it behind them and Cosmo opened the airlock's outer hatch, pulling himself aboard *Orpheus*. The space station's power was down and it had lost gravity. Cosmo and Nuri floated down a dark metal corridor, shining their plasma torches ahead of them.

Cosmo heard clanging sounds from the control room at the end of the corridor. He prised open its door and shone his torch inside. It was drenched in green slime and there was a huge hole in the ceiling where a metal panel had been torn off.

The light from Cosmo and Nuri's torches revealed the wolf-headed man in the oxygen mask. He was trying desperately to fix the melting control desk. His eyes looked wild with fright.

"We're from G-Watch," Cosmo said. "We've come to help you."

"Oh, thank goodness," the man replied, his voice sounding muffled beneath the mask. "My name is Provix, and I'm *Orpheus*'s captain. The space station was attacked by a monster – some kind of enormous fanged alien."

"That alien's called Zillah," Cosmo explained.

"It tore *Orpheus* apart and injected green slime into the hull. It's dissolving the supercomputer!"

Nuri shone her plasma torch on the control desk and examined the green liquid. "This looks like some kind of acidic saliva capable of digesting metal," she said.

"You have to help me get the supercomputer working again," Captain Provix said desperately. "There's a convoy of eight cargo freighters travelling through the Tarn Belt right now. Without *Orpheus*'s navigation system to guide them, they'll never make it past the asteroids."

Cosmo could see the control desk bubbling and dissolving before his very eyes. He glanced at Nuri gravely, who shook her head.

"It's no use," she said. "We'd need new parts to fix the computer."

"Captain Provix, where did the alien go?" Cosmo asked.

"It went into the Tarn Belt too," Provix replied. "It fired a cable to an asteroid and swung away on it."

"A cable?"

"A white cable, like a spider's thread."

A loud creaking noise came from the ship's hull as the last rivets that were holding it together began to pop out.

"Captain Provix, we have to get you out of here," Cosmo said. "This place is breaking up. Does *Orpheus* have an escape pod?"

"Yes, it's back down the corridor," Provix said. "But what about the freighters?"

"Nuri and I will go after the freighters, Captain – and the alien too. Now, let's go!"

Cosmo pulled Captain Provix out of the control room and down the dark corridor, floating in zero gravity. Nuri shone her torch on the hatch to the escape pod.

Cosmo opened it and helped the captain into a small torpedo-like capsule.

"Thank you," Provix said. "Good luck."

Cosmo closed the hatch. Instantly the pod fired away from the stricken space station onto the Great Western Tradeway, the force of its blast causing the corridor to shudder. There was a wrenching sound of metal and Cosmo felt the walls trembling. "Quick, Nuri, back to the Dragster!"

The corridor was collapsing around them as they pulled themselves along. They clambered through the Dragster's hatch, then burst back up into the cockpit.

"Brain-E, thrusters on!" Cosmo yelled.

The brainbot fired up the Dragster, and Cosmo jumped into the pilot's seat, blasting them away from the space station as it split apart. Fragments of metal and glass went spinning away through space.

"That was close," Cosmo said.

"Way too close," Nuri added, brushing
green slime from her spacesuit sleeve.

"Nuri, could you radio G-Watch
headquarters and inform them that all
tradeway traffic is to stay out of the Tarn
Asteroid Belt until instructed otherwise?"

"Right away," Nuri replied, reaching
for the ship's communicator.

Brain-E bleeped. "But with the Tradeway at a standstill, the whole of the galaxy will suffer, Master Cosmo. Supplies won't get through and food will quickly run out."

Cosmo glanced at the space traffic jam. *That's why Kaos beamed Zillah here*, he thought. *We have to stop her!*

He looked towards the Tarn Belt, its asteroids swirling menacingly. "Zillah's in there somewhere, Nuri, and so is the convoy of freighters."

"They're in danger," Nuri replied.

Cosmo accelerated towards the vast swirling mass, and the warning flashed on the screen once more: DANGER! TARN ASTEROID BELT! DO NOT ENTER!

Brain-E's bug-like eyes extended on metal stalks, peering nervously out through the spacescreen. "Master Cosmo, you're not going to fly into the Tarn Belt unguided, are you? If those asteroids collide with the Dragster, they'll split us open like a tin can."

"We have no choice, Brain-E," Cosmo replied, tapping the spacescreen and

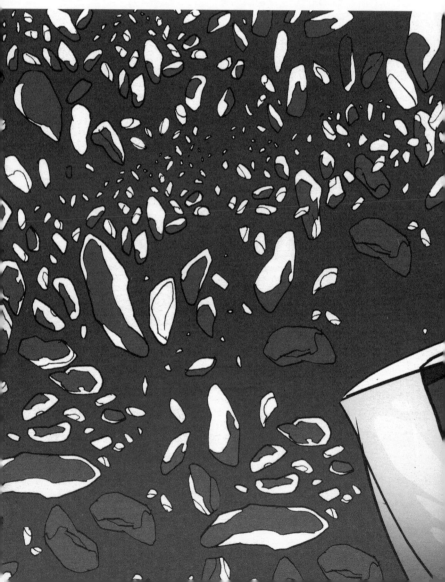

switching off the star plotter's warning. He scanned his instruments, making sure he was ready. "Hold on tight. We're going in!"

Can Cosmo make it through the Asteroid Belt? Find out in ZILLAH – THE FANGED PREDATOR . . .

WORDSEARCH

Reading across, up, down, diagonally and backwards, see if you can find all the listed words in the grid below.

A	G	P	Q	N	X	B	F	I	R	U	N
T	U	A	Z	U	J	E	A	E	N	A	O
C	H	L	R	U	H	T	T	T	E	U	P
O	L	M	Q	R	C	S	T	R	B	N	N
S	P	E	T	S	G	A	R	W	O	G	M
M	O	F	N	A	E	F	A	B	L	U	I
O	E	X	R	B	H	O	G	O	H	O	N
O	C	O	L	F	S	E	L	T	I	U	S
H	A	U	S	O	P	O	W	J	B	U	I
S	P	O	A	N	D	R	O	I	D	O	S
Z	S	K	K	X	K	A	U	B	G	O	F

Words: Garr; Cosmo; suit; Dragster; hogohon; vortex; android; Nuri; space; Kaos

CODE BREAKER

G1 has an urgent message for Cosmo. Can you break the code?

2/18/6/10 25/18/10

____ ___

21/22/20/26/21/22/21 6/5 25/26/10

_____ __ ___

5/22/15/11 11/18/9/24/22/11.

____ _____

21/18/5/24/22/9 26/4/4/26/5/22/5/11

_____ _____

26/5 24/18/4/4/18 8/12/18/21/9/18/5/11!

__ _____ _____!

Key:

1	2	3	4	5	6	7	8	9	10	11	12	13
J	K	L	M	N	O	P	Q	R	S	T	U	V

14	15	16	17	18	19	20	21	22	23	24	25	26
W	X	Y	Z	A	B	C	D	E	F	G	H	I

253

QUESTION CHALLENGE

Have you read ROCKHEAD and INFERNOX closely? See if you can answer these questions.

1. What is the name of Cosmo's Space Studies teacher?

2. How many arms does Graplax have?

3. What is Kaos's battleship called?

4. What speed must Cosmo travel when he enters Garr's atmosphere?

5. Nuri saves Cosmo's life with what type of pollen?

6. What type of tree does the tree sloth hide in?

7. Where does Magmus the lavabear originate from?

8. How many miles away is Planet Zaman from G-Watch HQ?

ANSWERS: 1. Mr Marshall; 2. Six; 3. Oblivion; 4. Four vectrons; 5. Yellowbell; 6. Glimpan tree; 7. Planet Vulcana; 8. 2.6 billion

254

WORD SCRAMBLE

Can you unscramble these words to reveal
a secret message from Kaos?

YM ILEAN VRDAESIN
ERA STUNPALBPOE.
THIW METH, I LIWL
YOTREDS H-GAWCT
NAD EKAT EVOR HET
YALGAX!

__ _____ _____

___ _____.

_____ ____—, _ ____

_____ _-_____

___ ____ _____ ___

_____!

NOW IT'S YOUR TURN TO DO BATTLE!

Have you collected the
ALIEN INVADERS gaming cards?

In the first five books you'll find these twenty gaming cards plus two bonus cards that you can download from the **ALIEN INVADERS** website

ROCKHEAD

Rockhead the living mountain comes from the barren planet of Cajon, and battles Cosmo at G-Watch headquarters.

INTELLIGENCE	22
SPEED	65
STRENGTH	100
FREAK FACTOR	55
POWER OF THE UNIVERSE	60

HAMMERFIST

Hammerfist is an Ogron from Planet Ajax, with an iron punch that can knock out his opponents.

INTELLIGENCE	30
SPEED	51
STRENGTH	88
FREAK FACTOR	60
POWER OF THE UNIVERSE	52

MUCOSA

Mucosa, a slugoid from Planet Agar, has sliming glands all over his body, enabling him to trap enemies with his sticky slime.

INTELLIGENCE	54
SPEED	8
STRENGTH	15
FREAK FACTOR	95
POWER OF THE UNIVERSE	48

COSMO

Cosmo, an Earthling boy, possesses the Power of the Universe, and can use the Quantum Mutation Suit to transform into any alien form.

INTELLIGENCE	95
SPEED	60
STRENGTH	60
FREAK FACTOR	70
POWER OF THE UNIVERSE	100

INFERNOX

Infernox comes from Redzin-5, an ever-expanding sun in the Doom Vortex, and has the ability to hurl fireballs and breathe fire.

INTELLIGENCE	58
SPEED	65
STRENGTH	75
FREAK FACTOR	77
POWER OF THE UNIVERSE	65

KAOS

Kaos is a five-headed alien outlaw with one goal: to take control of the galaxy.

INTELLIGENCE	90
SPEED	22
STRENGTH	32
FREAK FACTOR	85
POWER OF THE UNIVERSE	40

MAGMUS

A lava bear from Planet Vulcana, Magmus has explosive strength and heat-resistant armour plating to protect himself from attack.

INTELLIGENCE	35
SPEED	70
STRENGTH	70
FREAK FACTOR	59
POWER OF THE UNIVERSE	50

DECAGORG

Decagorg is a mega-squid from Planet Seamar. He is able to swim fast underwater and is armed with six grappling tentacles.

INTELLIGENCE	55
SPEED	80
STRENGTH	60
FREAK FACTOR	48
POWER OF THE UNIVERSE	55

www.**ALIENINVADERS**.co.uk

ZILLAH

Zillah is a female scavenger from the Doom Vortex who feeds on space wreckage in the vortex's treacherous storm zones.

INTELLIGENCE	75
SPEED	70
STRENGTH	75
FREAK FACTOR	85
POWER OF THE UNIVERSE	70

☐

NURI

Nuri, a blue-skinned Etrusian girl, is a G-Watch agent and co-pilot to Cosmo on his missions to defeat the alien invaders.

INTELLIGENCE	85
SPEED	55
STRENGTH	55
FREAK FACTOR	59
POWER OF THE UNIVERSE	65

☐

LASARG

An Argonite from Planet Kova, Lasarg has laser-eyes than he can use as devastating weapons.

INTELLIGENCE	70
SPEED	50
STRENGTH	40
FREAK FACTOR	75
POWER OF THE UNIVERSE	70

☐

LUCONA

A star fly from the Jittasian Star Nursery, Lucona is small but very powerful, and glows with the brightness of a brand-new star.

INTELLIGENCE	10
SPEED	75
STRENGTH	5
FREAK FACTOR	85
POWER OF THE UNIVERSE	85

☐

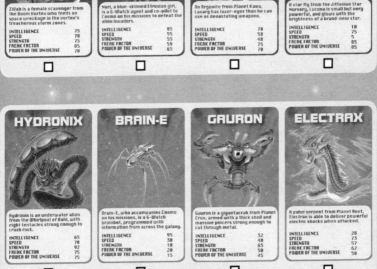

HYDRONIX

Hydronix is an underwater alien from the Whirlpool of Dahl, with eight tentacles strong enough to crush rock.

INTELLIGENCE	65
SPEED	70
STRENGTH	92
FREAK FACTOR	70
POWER OF THE UNIVERSE	75

☐

BRAIN-E

Brain-E, who accompanies Cosmo on his missions, is a G-Watch brainoid, programmed with information from across the galaxy.

INTELLIGENCE	95
SPEED	50
STRENGTH	10
FREAK FACTOR	20
POWER OF THE UNIVERSE	15

☐

GAURON

Gauron is a gigantacrab from Planet Crux, armed with a thick shell and massive pincers strong enough to cut through metal.

INTELLIGENCE	52
SPEED	40
STRENGTH	65
FREAK FACTOR	50
POWER OF THE UNIVERSE	45

☐

ELECTRAX

A pulse serpent from Planet Beet, Electrax is able to deliver powerful electric shocks when attacked.

INTELLIGENCE	28
SPEED	75
STRENGTH	57
FREAK FACTOR	62
POWER OF THE UNIVERSE	50

☐

ATOMIC

Atomic comes from a radioactive star in the heart of the Doom Vortex. He can detonate himself and reform, like a living bomb.

INTELLIGENCE	55
SPEED	40
STRENGTH	95
FREAK FACTOR	100
POWER OF THE UNIVERSE	70

☐

G1

G1, the silver-eyed chief of G-Watch, is from the ancient planet of Oracion, and protects the galaxy from invasion.

INTELLIGENCE	100
SPEED	40
STRENGTH	57
FREAK FACTOR	59
POWER OF THE UNIVERSE	95

☐

FREEZOTH

An ice-serpent from Planet Perfidian, Freezoth resembles a dragon with cold-resistant scales and a freezing breath of -273.25°C.

INTELLIGENCE	55
SPEED	42
STRENGTH	40
FREAK FACTOR	63
POWER OF THE UNIVERSE	51

☐

CHOD

Chod is an Bardgark from Planet Rudron. He has a metal exoskeleton that defends him against even the most powerful explosions.

INTELLIGENCE	42
SPEED	25
STRENGTH	75
FREAK FACTOR	55
POWER OF THE UNIVERSE	38

☐

NOW YOU CAN PLAY ALIEN INVADERS TOO . . .

HOW TO PLAY
ALIEN INVADERS

Challenge a friend to do battle.

Shuffle the cards and deal them equally between you.

Look at your top card and choose a category.

If the value for that category is higher than your opponent's, you win their card.

If the value is lower, they win your card and pick the next category.

If the values are the same, then put the cards in a pile and play another round: the winner takes all the cards in the pile.

The champion is the first to win all the cards.

Pick a category

How powerful are you?

G1, the silver-eyed chief of G-Watch, is from the ancient planet of Oraclon, and protects the galaxy from invasion.

INTELLIGENCE	100
SPEED	40
STRENGTH	57
FREAK FACTOR	59
POWER OF THE UNIVERSE	95

GOOD LUCK!
THE POWER OF THE UNIVERSE IS IN YOU!

ABOUT THE AUTHOR

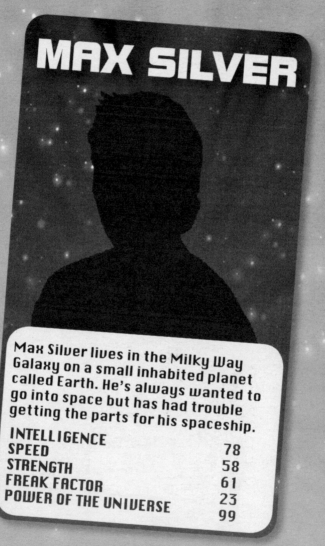

MAX SILVER

Max Silver lives in the Milky Way Galaxy on a small inhabited planet called Earth. He's always wanted to go into space but has had trouble getting the parts for his spaceship.

INTELLIGENCE	78
SPEED	58
STRENGTH	61
FREAK FACTOR	23
POWER OF THE UNIVERSE	99